COVEN

SHORT STORIES BUNDLE, VOL. 1

DAVID NETH

DN Publishing

Subscribe to the author's newsletter for updates and exclusive content:
DavidNethBooks.com/Newsletter

Follow the author at:
www.facebook.com/DavidNethBooks

Also by David Neth

Lost by Magic
Lost By Magic
Lucky By Magic
Lured By Magic

Coven
Harpy
Siren
Valkyrie
Shapeshifter
Sorcerer
Witch (Short Story)
Enchantress
Oracle
Trickster
Poltergeist
Hex (Short Story)
Witch Hunter
Demon (Short Story)

Under the Moon
The Full Moon
The Harvest Moon
The Blood Moon
The Crescent Moon
The Blue Moon

The Art of Magic

Fuse
Origin
Omertá
Oblivion

Heat
Black Magnet
Dust Storm
The Gatekeeper

Standalone
All I Ever Wanted

AUTHOR'S NOTE

These short stories were written because I had so many ideas for stories about the Coven characters floating in my head and, honestly, some of the storylines didn't fit into a full-length book. Nonetheless, I wanted these stories to be told and be included in a part of the Art of Magic universe that I've created over the years.

As you are already well aware, this book is a collection of short stories from throughout the series. Meaning that these stories jump around chronologically throughout the series.

The first short story in this collection is *Witch*, which takes place between *Sorcerer* (Book 5) and *Enchantress* (Book 6), immediately after Samantha and Steven get married. This story also ties in storylines that were touched on in *The Harvest Moon*, which is the second book in the Under the Moon series, and is an important piece of the puzzle to the Art of Magic universe.

The second short story is *Hex*, which takes place between *Poltergeist* (Book 9) and *Witch Hunter* (Book 10). This is a short, fun, quirky story that I wanted to tell simply because I thought it would be fun to do. I wanted to show more of the playful banter between the sisters and put them in a magically awkward situation with people who have no idea that magic exists. In this story, you'll note that Samantha is very pregnant, which is a big jump from *Witch*, where she first learns that she's pregnant. Again, it comes down to the chronology of the series as a whole and *Hex*'s placement in that chronology.

The third and final story in this collection is *Demon*, which is a story that I knew I wanted to write as soon as I decided to do a Samantha-only story with *Witch*. This story takes place a week after the events of *Witch Hunter* (Book 10). In this story, Kathy is the main focus, because Samantha is taking time to be a mother to her newborn son. With both *Witch* and *Demon*, I thought it would be important to show the dynamics between the sisters individually in contrast to how they are together in the full-length books. As you will read in these short stories, each sister struggles on her own, even if she is ultimately able to "save the day" at the end. What they both learn, however, is that they're better together than they are separately.

As you read, pay attention to the dates and the order that these stories play in the overall series (and the overall universe). I hope you enjoy them! There is a lot more coming for the Harper/Bowen witches!

- David Neth

FROM THE AUTHOR OF THE UNDER THE MOON SERIES

DAVID NETH

Don't go looking
for trouble.

WITCH

COVEN: BOOK 5.5

CHAPTER 1

- JANUARY 27, 1989 -
FRIDAY

If I die out here, nobody will even know where to look for me, Samantha thought as she lurked behind a stack of wooden pallets.

She was outside an abandoned warehouse on an unlit side street in Salem, NY, which was essentially right on the border with Vermont. She had been attending an accounting conference in nearby Saratoga Springs when she decided to take the detour east to find one witch in particular. When she arrived, however, she stumbled on something else brewing.

Inside the abandoned warehouse, Samantha could sense a negative energy. She didn't know what it was, but she didn't dare enter. Danielle Bowen, the witch she had come to Salem to see, was currently standing on top of another stack of pallets beside the warehouse, peeking through a hole in the metal siding where an air vent had fallen out. Samantha thought it was best to hold her hidden position until something else happened.

It didn't take long. Danielle slipped on the pallets and her knee slammed against the metal siding, sending echoes ricocheting down the length of the wall.

Samantha further retreated into the shadows as Danielle struggled to regain her balance before she climbed down. When she finally did, two figures approached her from the front of the building. Likely the ones Danielle had been eavesdropping on.

From her hiding spot behind the pallets, Samantha could make out that it was a man and a woman as they came closer. The man looked like a typical demonic thug: dark hair, tribal tattoos up and down his arms, and broad shoulders that she figured he often used to intimidate everyone he came in contact with.

The woman with him, on the other hand, was most notable for her bright green hair. She wore body armor and bracelets on both wrists. Over her shoulder was a fur shall to keep her warm in the cold.

"I suppose I need to work on my hiding places," the woman said. She stepped closer to Danielle, who was pressed against the stack of pallets. "While you're here, I'd like to introduce you to my husband, Dragonox."

"Husband?" There was surprise in Danielle's voice.

"I've just been telling him all about your family and what

your grandmother did to me all those years ago, and I seem to have gotten him riled up." The woman now had one hand leaning on the pallet just above Danielle's shoulder, further pinning her in place.

Samantha watched, waiting for the perfect time to step in and help Danielle. For the moment, though, it seemed she had the element of surprise and she didn't want to ruin that.

"And what a surprise that you're here," the green-haired woman went on. "Unfortunately for me, I have plans with Dragonox, and I can't kill you myself."

Samantha looked around to make sure nobody was sneaking up on her. She would be no help to Danielle if she was jumped herself.

"I have some friends that can take care of you themselves."

The woman raised her free hand, and water rose up from the frozen ground, puddling in three different places around her. The puddles stretched upward and from them, bodies formed into three distinct figures. Within seconds, the puddles had come alive, and each took on the form of a person.

"Enjoy!" The green-haired woman smiled and patted Danielle's cheek. Turning, she walked off with her brute of a companion.

Samantha searched around her for something to use as a weapon. Finally, she noted a loose board that had fallen from one of the pallets and she ran around to assist Danielle, but she was gone.

WITCH

Looking around, Samantha tried to lay eyes on her in the darkness, but the sound of her groaning gave away her location from the back of the warehouse.

Breaking into a run, Samantha dashed down to the back wall of the building and came around the corner, where Danielle was blocked into a dead-end by a broken-down utility truck.

Soon after Samantha rounded the corner, the water creatures had overpowered Danielle, knocking her to the ground, where she gargled on the water being forced down her throat.

Quickly, Samantha thought up a simple, two-line spell:

> *From the liquid you were born,*
> *I turn you now to solid form.*

The creatures lurched as their bodies turned gray and solidified. Sensing the change, Danielle delivered a satisfying kick into the stomach of one.

Samantha ran up and smacked one on the back of the head, where it splashed back into a puddle and fell to the ground. Spinning around, Samantha kicked the third figure in its side, where it hit the metal siding of the building and splattered like a water balloon bursting.

Turning down to Danielle, Samantha offered her hand to help the witch up.

Back on her feet, Danielle turned back to the creatures, who had all reformed. She extended her palms to them and ice crystals shot out of her open hands, freezing the creatures in place. Samantha wound up her swing with the plank and shattered them to pieces.

"Thank you!" Danielle said breathlessly. "I was a little scared for a minute."

Samantha smiled and tossed the plank aside. "My pleasure."

Danielle extended her hand. "I'm Danielle Bowen. Who are you?"

"I'm Samantha Harper." Samantha could tell that Danielle seemed nervous about the introduction, but she quickly tried to hide it.

"Nice to meet you." Danielle brushed off the dirt from her jeans. "Are you from Salem?"

"Oh, no. I actually came here to see you." Samantha moved her hair out of her face as a cold breeze moved through.

"Me?"

She nodded. "You do readings, right?"

Danielle looked at her watch and Samantha realized just how late it was: Going on ten o'clock at night. She had wanted to get here earlier, but she and the other staff members from Darius Wilcox, CPA, had gone to dinner together, then out for drinks, which Samantha abstained from. It was nearly nine before she had gotten on the road.

"Uh, yeah," Danielle said. "But this is a little after my typical business hours."

"I know," Samantha said quickly. "I'm sorry. But you're the only psychic that I could find who I suspected was an actual witch. I need a very definitive answer."

It was the line she had practiced to herself on her drive over. Help Danielle bring her guard down by asking her for something innocent like a psychic reading. Then she could move in with the real reason she wanted to see her.

Plus, she really did have a question she wanted answered. Something that had come up on her honeymoon earlier in the week.

Danielle nodded. "Um…okay." She hesitated, then added, "Why don't we head back down to my shop?"

Samantha followed her to Thomas Street, which connected to Main Street. There, the streetlights provided the safety both witches were looking for. Samantha also noted that her car was the last one parked on the street. She hoped there were no parking curfews. The last thing she needed was a ticket from a town on the whole other side of New York.

When they got to the shop, Danielle unlocked the front door and flicked on the lights. Once they were inside, she locked the door behind them. Samantha initially thought she was being paranoid, but the woman had also just been attacked down a dark street. She was probably more than a little shaken.

The shop was larger than Samantha had anticipated. The

building was definitely old, that was for sure, but it had an antiquated beauty in it that Samantha appreciated.

In the center of the room sat a round table with a white tablecloth. Lining the walls were shelves filled with the typical stock of most occult shops that Samantha had seen back in Erie. Dried herbs and books on spells, divination, and centering oneself. There were also trinkets and talismans and tokens that would seem like fun tchotchkes to anyone unfamiliar with the world of magic.

"Take a seat." Danielle pointed to the table. "I have to make a phone call." She disappeared through a door behind the checkout counter.

In her absence, Samantha looked around at the items in the shop. She was surprised to see a collection of athames, which were ceremonial knives used in rituals and other spells. At Mystic Treasures in Erie, Samantha knew that the owners kept those items behind the counter for safekeeping, and yet here Danielle had hers on full display.

She had just moved on to examining the dried herbs in the jars when she heard the door squeak, signaling Danielle's return.

"You have an impressive stock here," Samantha said. "I wish I had a store like this back in Erie." It was her way of slipping in her location into the conversation. A way to further disarm Danielle.

"Erie? Like Pennsylvania? Is that where you're from?"

Samantha nodded. "Yep. My great-grandparents built a house there a long time ago. It's been in the family ever since."

Danielle nodded politely. "Why don't we sit?" After she took her own seat, she reached for her tarot cards and began shuffling them.

Samantha sat across from Danielle and studied her. She couldn't determine exactly what was on Danielle's mind from social cues, and she didn't want to use her telepathic abilities to eavesdrop. That would be a last resort. She had survived this long without mind-reading, she wasn't going to start doing it willy-nilly and invading people's privacy. Danielle had every right to be hesitant.

"I'm a good witch, you know," Samantha added, knowing that words only meant so much in this situation. "You don't have to be scared. I fight evil." She chuckled. "*Lots* of evil—with my sister. I know what you must be thinking. And I also know that my telling you to trust me isn't going to make you trust me, but I figure it's better to say it anyway."

Danielle didn't appear to hear her. Instead, she took a deep breath and set the deck on the table. "Cut the deck."

Samantha split the deck into thirds. "My sister and I have taken quite a beating throughout our magical careers. We have also taken out quite a few bad guys. As I'm sure you know, we've had some unexpected attacks, some unexpected deaths—"

"What's your point?" The abruptness of Danielle's words caught Samantha by surprise. Danielle didn't appear angry.

Scared, maybe, but not obviously so. Samantha resisted the temptation to push into Danielle's mind.

"My husband and I got married earlier this year." Samantha eased into her story. She didn't want to seem like a lovelorn honeymooner, so she made the details a bit more ambiguous. "Earlier this year" was true in the sense that she got married at the start of 1989…even if that was only two weeks ago. Samantha hoped that Danielle assumed she meant the beginning of 1988, which would further add credence to the story Samantha was about to spin.

"And now he's talking about having kids," Samantha went on, "and I don't know if that's a good idea."

The statement in itself was not a total lie. Steven had brought up the idea of starting a family during their stay in the Pocono Mountains, reasoning that since they were married they should start talking about the next step so they could properly prepare. Samantha had distracted him by saying she wanted to be a wife for a little bit before she considered being a mother too.

The truth was, she was nervous to bring kids into their lives. While it was true that they hadn't had a major magical attack in a while, she and Kathy could never predict when the next one was about to strike. Would Samantha's baby be in the crosshairs of an unexpected attack?

"Is your husband magical?" Danielle fussed with something beneath the table and came up with two candles: red and green.

Samantha shook her head. "No. And since we've been married he's managed to stay out of the line of fire, so it's possible our kids will too. I'm just afraid that they won't. Or they'll be targeted. Or I'll be taken from them before they can really remember me." For a moment, Samantha almost forgot that she was talking to a stranger. Danielle felt like an old friend, even though they had just met.

Danielle cleared her throat. "So you came here all the way from Erie to get a reading from me?"

"Yes."

"Okay," Danielle muttered to herself.

Samantha could hear the doubt in Danielle's voice and she wondered if she was about to be thrown out. Or possibly worse.

Instead, Danielle proceeded with the reading. She drew from the decks, placing them around the table and studying each one. She frowned.

"Let's try a different method." Danielle reached behind her and pulled out a notebook from the bookshelf behind the table. After flipping through a couple of the pages, she held her finger down to one and said, "We're going to try a spell. Since you're a witch too, it should be a stronger connection. Have you ever done any divination spells?"

Samantha shook her head. "No. My sister has dabbled, but I haven't. I'm more into potions."

"You're a lot like my husband then." Danielle again fished several more candles from the box. This time they were purple, silver, and gray. Samantha knew the colors had meaning, but she couldn't remember what they symbolized off the top of her head.

"He's really good in the kitchen," Danielle said.

Samantha smiled politely.

Danielle arranged the candles until they were in the sign of a pentagram. After that, she used blue yarn to connect them to one another. This was already more complicated than any spell or ritual Samantha and Kathy had casted before. Samantha was impressed with Danielle's knowledge.

The witch extended her arms across the table to Samantha. "Take my hands and say this spell with me."

With the candles burning between their locked hands, the witches recited together:

> *Magical divinity,*
> *show me what I need to see.*

Over and over again, they repeated the spell. With each run, the air in the room began to stir, building with intensity. Both witches concentrated on the spell and combining their energies.

Suddenly, the flames of the candles shot up straight in the air, causing Samantha to close her eyes reflexively. She could feel the heat licking her hands. Nothing too intense, but enough to know that the wind was whipping the flames around too.

Abruptly, the wind ceased as the witches were thrown away

from each other. Even though Samantha heard the crash, she was locked in a vision that captured her full attention.

Samantha saw a cluttered attic that looked very similar to hers, but it was subtly different. She didn't frequent her attic much, but she could tell that the one in her vision wasn't the one she had left back in Erie. There was more furniture, additional boxes; some labeled "Josh," others labeled "Chris," whoever they were. Overall, despite the added storage, the space seemed tidier than Samantha remembered.

Curiously, everything in the attic appeared to have been sprayed down with a hose or something similar. Each of the rafters dripped with water and boxes sagged from the moisture. Dirt and dust clung together in puddles.

What Samantha focused on, however, was the teenaged girl with long black hair knelt on the floor over a teenaged boy wearing a black jacket. In his hands was *The Art of Magic*, which he flipped through rapidly. His face was panicked, clearly in distress over a coming attack or some other crisis.

Samantha's mind spun as she tried to make sense of it all. Were these her kids? Was this vision trying to tell her that her kids would be facing the same dangers she and Kathy did? Judging by the way the boy flipped through the book, he wasn't used to finding what he needed in it. And his alarmed look only worried Samantha. Why wouldn't her children be prepared as witches?

That was, if these teenagers even *were* her children. Maybe they were Danielle's. But what were they doing in Samantha's house?

From across the room, Samantha saw the green-haired woman from the warehouse step into the attic. The boy shoved the book toward the girl and stood in front of her. If these were Samantha's kids, at least she could count on them to protect each other.

Just as quickly as the vision came, suddenly it was gone. Samantha opened her eyes. Danielle was already on her feet, standing across the room examining a journal of some sort.

"What happened?" Samantha asked.

Danielle looked at Samantha with wide eyes. "I think you just discovered a prophecy."

CHAPTER 2

"A prophecy?" Samantha pinched the bridge of her nose and closed her eyes as she sat up. "But I don't get visions."

Danielle shook her head. "Neither do I. But I got one too."

Samantha raised an eyebrow. "You're a psychic."

"I read cards."

Samantha looked around the shop. The wind and the blast from the spell had trashed everything. All the delicately-placed items on the shelves were strewn about. Some of the jars of herbs were cracked. Books were turned over. Whole shelves had been shattered into splinters.

Danielle held out a pad of paper and a pen to her. "Here. Write down the prophecy while it's still fresh in your mind."

Samantha was confused. This was all moving too fast. She hadn't ever come in contact with prophecies before, so she wasn't positive that that's what this was. "I don't even remember what I said."

Danielle let out a heavy sigh and turned her attention to the pad of paper. She began scribbling on it with the pen, likely writing the prophecy herself. When she finished, she flipped the page and rewrote it on a second piece. After that, she ripped the top page off and handed it to Samantha.

"Here. Add this to your collection of spells, wherever you keep it." Danielle got to her feet and stepped to the counter. She pushed aside sheets of paper scattered all along the wooden top until she snatched up a leather-bound journal.

Samantha glanced at the chicken scratch Danielle had added to the paper:

When the sun is black and the moon is red, a man will emerge from the shadows to triumphantly spread the darkness.

She stepped up to the customer side of the counter and looked around at more of the damage. "Sorry about your shop."

Danielle wrote quickly into her journal and waved off Samantha's comment. "I can clean it up."

After watching for a moment, Samantha asked, "What do

you think happened? I've never experienced anything like that before."

Danielle held up her finger after finishing in her journal. "I have an idea. Whether that's what happened or not is to be decided, but I'm guessing that combining our magic with the incense in the room set off a magical reaction that caused both of us to experience a special phenomenon. Neither one of us have had visions before, yet that's exactly what happened." She indicated the prophecy that she had transcribed into her journal. "This was destined to happen. Now we just need to figure out why."

"Okay…" Samantha slowly, stalling for time. She was both impressed and intimidated by Danielle's knowledge of magic. Trickles of doubt creeped into her mind asking, *Could I really trust her?* "But how did a simple reading about whether I should have kids or not trigger this? This prophecy doesn't even mention my kids."

Danielle used her finger to tap her lips as she thought. "Maybe—and I'm just spitballing here—but maybe this prophecy isn't meant for us. It's meant for our kids."

"Do you have kids?" Samantha thought it might be easier to trust a mother.

"No."

"Then how does that make sense?"

"I don't know!"

Samantha tucked her hair behind both ears and crossed her

arms. She tried her best to control her frustration. She could tell they were both still nervous about revealing all of their secrets to each other, so instead they were dancing around half-truths that didn't resolve anything. "Okay, let's forget the prophecy for a moment. We each had a vision. What did you see?"

Danielle paused and took a deep breath. "I was in some sort of attic. Lots of clutter, high ceilings—maybe an old Victorian house?"

Samantha nodded.

"Toxan—a woman with green hair was there, and so were two kids," Danielle went on. "Maybe midteens? A boy and a girl. The girl...I don't know what it is, but I just have this strong connection to her. This feeling that she's..."

Samantha focused her eyes on Danielle, fighting every temptation to let her persuasion influence the discussion. If Danielle sensed that Samantha was using magic, the delicate trust that they were forming would be shattered.

As it stood, it was obvious that Danielle was keeping something from her anyway.

"I don't know, exactly," Danielle finally said. "Just a connection somehow."

"Oh." Samantha paused, hoping that Danielle would add more, but she didn't. If Danielle was going to tell her anything, Samantha needed to offer a little more insight into her own life to continue that trust. "Well that messy attic is probably mine. Like I said, the house has been in the family awhile, so I don't think it's going anywhere."

Danielle didn't respond at first. Her eyes shifted down to the cluttered countertop as she became lost in thought.

"Do you know who the green-haired woman is?" Samantha asked gently, hoping not to scare her off. But the woman—the same one they saw at the warehouse—was in the vision they both shared.

Danielle nodded. "Aside from tarot reading, she's about the only thing my family has shared over the years."

A common enemy that lasted generations. Sometimes Samantha wondered how close she and Kathy would be if they didn't have shared enemies knocking on their door all the time. Certainly now that she was married, Samantha knew she would probably feel the same way Steven did: wanting to get their own place away from Kathy.

But that's not what their lives were like.

"So do you think that my question about having children was somehow transferred to you?" Samantha asked.

Danielle looked up, confused. "What do you mean?"

Samantha raised an eyebrow. "If the question about me being able to have kids resulted in a vision of two kids I have no connection to, then they've gotta be yours." She smiled and decided to press her luck. "Were those kids *your* kids?"

"I don't know. The boy definitely wasn't. I didn't feel any sort of connection to him. But the girl..." She shook her head. "There's no way to prove it. Probably, though. But the vision isn't set in stone, either. Sure, it showed that I have a daughter, but that can change in the future. I could run out and get hit by a car on my way home and never bear any children."

Samantha shook her head. "If our visions were destined, that's not going to happen."

"Very true. I guess I'm just confused as to why that vision triggered the prophecy from you," Danielle said. "It was my daughter and my family enemy. It just happened to be in your house."

Samantha shrugged. "Maybe they aren't connected? Maybe the vision was meant for you, but the prophecy was meant for me?"

"Then why did we both see the vision but only you spoke the prophecy?"

Samantha threw up her hands, her temper finally getting the better of her. "I don't know! I came here to ask whether it's safe to have kids, and we opened up a whole can of worms with this mess."

"Are you sure that's the reason?"

Samantha's heart began to race. "I don't understand what you're suggesting."

Danielle rolled her eyes and put one hand on her hip. "Why don't you just tell me what you really came for?"

"What do you mean?"

"Oh, come on! You came all the way from your big city to some Podunk town because I'm suddenly the best there is for your vanity question?" Danielle shook her head. "I don't believe it. There have got to be other witches in Erie or some other place between here and there that you could've asked."

Samantha bristled at being found out. And she didn't think asking about the safety of her potential children was a vanity question. "I wanted you."

"Why? There are plenty of mediums in Lily Dale, or any of the major cities in Pennsylvania or New York. Why come to Salem? What is it about this place—or me—that drew you here?" Danielle's stare was intense.

Samantha crossed her arms and held the witch's gaze. "I'm aware of Toxanna, and I've heard of your family."

"How?"

"In the demonic world. She's very happy that she has never lost. My condolences for your family, by the way."

Truth was, Samantha's honeymoon had almost been ruined by a demonic encounter. At the resort they had been staying at in the Pocono Mountains, Samantha overheard a demon trying to swindle the girl behind the front desk into emptying the cash drawer.

Samantha had done some brief mind-reading to be certain that it was a demon—or some other magical enemy. In his head, she uncovered chatter about an evil witch targeting a family of witches in Upstate New York. He knew her name was Toxanna and in his thoughts, Samantha stumbled on his hope to work with her.

That ended quickly when Samantha managed to persuade him outside into a private area. She wasn't the spell master of the family, although she managed to come up with a banishment spell to get rid of the demon. But the knowledge of Toxanna still weighed on her.

When she was asked at work to go the conference in Saratoga Springs, only about a forty-five minute drive from Salem, Samantha jumped at the chance. Even though it meant cutting her honeymoon a day short.

"How do you know about what is talked about in the demonic world?" Danielle asked nervously.

Samantha shook her head to try to reassure her. "I'm telepathic. Some of the evils my sister and I fight have weak minds, and I've read some thoughts related to you and your family."

Best to keep the fact that she was a family woman at the forefront. If Samantha had told her the truth, about how she stumbled on the demon, she figured Danielle wouldn't trust her as much.

"Toxanna knows you're here," Samantha added.

Danielle nodded. "I discovered that today. Apparently she's a newlywed. But why does my family's tragedy even concern you?"

"Now it's my turn to hypothesize." Samantha dropped her head for a moment. "Um, I think some of my enemies and some of your enemies have been working together. Or, at least, talking about working together."

"What do you mean?"

"My sister and I just defeated this harpy…coven, for lack of a better word." It had actually been about seven months ago, but that detail didn't matter so much. "Their leader, Wren, not only had typical harpy powers—flying, sharp talons, screeching—but she could also manipulate the wind."

Danielle shrugged. "So? Some Greek mythologies said that harpies could control the weather, specifically the wind."

Samantha shook her head. "Not any that I've come across. Maybe back when that mythology was written that was the case, but things change. Creatures evolve. Look at how far witches have come in the past four hundred years."

"Okay. So this harpy had control of the wind, so what?"

"What is Toxanna's specialty?"

"Specialty?"

Samantha nodded. "Yeah, each witch has a specialty."

"Uh…water, I guess."

"Interesting," Samantha muttered. It fit into the theory that she'd been considering for months. Ever since they had encountered Wren's powers. Evil beings were catching on that they were stronger together. They had begun to organize. And if they organized, they could potentially be unstoppable. "I think the organization is related to the elements."

"What organization?"

"The one Toxanna and a bunch of other people are

forming," Samantha blurted. Then added, "Or I think they are. But I know they choose their partners based off the elements."

"You got that from two bad guys?"

"I know there's more. There has to be. My sister doesn't believe me, either, so I've let it go with her. But I'm telling you, I'm on to something."

Kathy didn't seem bothered by Wren's ability to control the wind. And once she started taking college classes, she didn't welcome any additional stresses.

Samantha agreed with Kathy, especially as she planned her wedding. But now her wedding was over and the thought of Wren with additional abilities still weighed on her.

Danielle leaned on the counter and asked, "So what do you want me to do?"

"You said Toxanna has a husband?"

"Yeah, but I don't know what his powers are."

"Just…watch them. If his powers are element-based, he may be another member of this…group." It was the most Samantha could ask Danielle to do, especially if Toxanna had killed every other member of her family. She was still in defensive mode and was in no situation to start asking questions. "I wouldn't put it past anyone to try to monopolize it."

Worry came over Danielle's face. But she took a deep breath and nodded. "Okay. I'll stay. I'll watch them. But you need to keep me updated on your end. I've been chased out of too many towns by this woman. If I stay, she's going to note the change in pattern. That is going to put a bigger target on me and my husband."

"Of course, yeah," Samantha said. "I don't want you or anyone else in your family to get hurt."

Danielle averted her eyes.

"Do you have something I can write my number on?" Samantha asked.

They exchanged contact information. Samantha slipped the small scrap of paper in the pocket of her jeans.

"Once I get home, I'll send you everything I have come up with so you can tell me your thoughts," Samantha said. It was only thoughts and ideas, nothing concrete. But it was a start. "As we work through everything, we may have to find other witches who have been targeted by other members of this group. Find out what they know so we can learn more. But we have to be careful. Evil talks."

"What if we come across someone who wants to join this supergroup?"

"We'll have to stop them."

CHAPTER 3

- FEBRUARY 3, 1989 -
FRIDAY

No, ma'am, I'm calling to ask about any unusual disturbances happening in your area," Samantha said into the phone.

She was perched on the end of her and Steven's bed with a notepad on her lap. The phone sat in front of her on the mattress, its cord extended to the jack in the wall. She'd brought it up from the living room for some privacy.

"Where are you calling from?"

"It doesn't matter," Samantha said. "I'm looking for someone who might be causing some kind of trouble near you. Something to do with the earth or rocks or plants maybe. Something magical."

"I have no idea what you're talking about," the woman on

the other end said. "And if you'd be so kind, I would like to get back to my customers now."

"Wait, ma'am, please!"

The line went dead.

Samantha slammed the phone back in its cradle. There was ten bucks down the drain for long-distance. She'd been calling occult shops in northern California, where Petram had last been seen. Over the last week, she had found him by checking into extreme weather across the country—earthquakes, in this instance. Of course, thanks to her day job, she could only do so much in the short amount of time in the day she had.

Since Danielle ran an occult shop and had the day to do what she needed, Samantha suggested that she look into the unusual earthquakes on the west coast, which was how Danielle discovered Petram's name. Now it was Samantha's turn to do some work on this case they were building. If she could gather witches to help her and Danielle stop Petram before he got stronger, they could keep the balance between good and evil intact. Maybe even start to build some sort of nationwide army against this supergroup.

Of course, it would help if she could actually get ahold of witches in California without scaring them off over the phone. Samantha couldn't blame them. If a stranger called her asking about magic and witches but wouldn't give any personal details, she wouldn't give them the time of day either.

"Are you still up here racking up our phone bill?" Steven

stepped into the room and took a seat beside his wife. "Dinner's just about ready."

Samantha glanced at the clock. It was almost six o'clock. In California, that meant it was three o'clock. She still had a couple more hours before the shops closed up for the night. But she was running out of shops to try.

"I have some more places to call," she said, indicating her list. She'd called an operator and got the names and phone numbers of several different shops in California, north of San Fransisco where the earthquakes had happened. She'd called a little more than half of them.

"Any luck so far?"

She shook her head. "Most places don't want to talk to me. And if they do, they're trying to sell me something."

"You're not telling them who you are, are you?" Steven asked nervously. "The last thing we need is people tracking you down and knocking on our doorstep."

"I'm being careful, honey." She reached for the phone again.

"If you were truly being careful, you wouldn't go looking for trouble like this," he said, then added, "or hiding it from your sister."

Kathy was working evening shifts at the store five days a week, on top of her morning classes and cramming her homework in every spare moment. Samantha knew how stressed Kathy was, and she was proud of her sister for having some drive. She wasn't going to derail that focus by bringing this into Kathy's world. She knew her sister would jump at the chance to distract herself with magic.

"I'm not *hiding* it from Kathy," Samantha said. "I just don't want her involved. And don't give me that look!" She wagged her finger at him. "I am merely gaining intel. I'm not *acting* on anything until I talk to Danielle."

"And you're positive this woman is someone you can trust?"

"She has more invested than I do. She's lost her whole family to a woman we think might be joining this supergroup. If someone that powerful joins four other people who are equally powerful to create a coven, they'd be unstoppable. This is preventative work for the future."

Steven sighed. "You know how much I don't like you tracking all these people down, so I'm not going to say much more. But I will say this: you and your family should come before anyone else." He leaned forward and kissed the top of Samantha's head. "Ten more minutes and then dinner will be done."

She nodded, thinking about what he had said. "Okay. I'll be there. Just one more call."

CHAPTER 4

- FEBRUARY 5, 1989 -
SUNDAY

Samantha carried the phone up to her bedroom and plugged it into the jack in the wall. She sat in the antique chair by the window, which usually only served as a place to set her clothes for the next day. Lately, though, she'd been using it as her work station to figure out more about the supergroup.

The Pentad.

That's what Danielle had learned the group called themselves. At first, it seemed that Danielle had made significant progress in their research. She had found a witch in Phoenix, Arizona named Ebony who was the fire branch of the Pentad. Ebony had set a devastating fire to a whole section of the city as a way to flex her power. Fortunately for Danielle, that's how she found her.

WITCH

The phone on the table began to ring and Samantha immediately snatched it up. Danielle's phone calls came most days at just after five, like clockwork.

"Hello?"

"Hi Samantha, it's me," Danielle said on the other end.

"How've you been? How's the shop?"

"Good. Sales are decent. I need to get to ordering more supplies sometime this week. I've been busy checking into the Pentad."

"Anything new?" It's what Samantha had wanted to ask first, but she knew how short and impersonal she could be at times. It was one of the things she was working on about herself.

"Well, still no luck in confirming the water branch," she said. "But I did find the air branch."

"Really?" Samantha was happy to hear that, although a little guilty that she hadn't contributed much to the search. They had already determined that Petram was the earth branch out in California, but Samantha had been unable to locate him or send a warning to any witches out that way. It left her feeling a little discouraged.

"Yeah," Danielle went on. "A sorcerer in Worcester, near Boston. Her name's Tabitha. She whipped up a tornado that killed three people and I thought, that's not normal for the northeast. So I checked into it."

"Any luck tracking down witches in that area?" Samantha coiled the phone cord around her finger.

Danielle scoffed. "Those Massachusetts witches are so annoying!"

"I know. I've had the same luck with the witches in California," Samantha said. "It seems like Melody was the only one who knew about him—or rather, what he was involved in."

In a previous telephone conversation the week before, Danielle had recounted how she had contacted Petram's latest victim to obtain as much information as possible. As with all calls to the world of the dead, the conversation was short-lived and not very informative, other than the name of the Pentad.

"And it's not even like they're particularly scared, either," Danielle added. "They just plain don't believe me."

"What do you mean?" Outside, a couple walked their dog on the sidewalk in the growing darkness.

"They're the hippy-dippy witches more worried about being centered and not disturbing the calm of all around them than they are about good and evil."

Samantha grinned. Danielle reminded her of Kathy in the way that she said what was on her mind.

"Which, by the way," Danielle went on, "they said they don't believe in. I didn't know you *could* believe in good and evil! I thought it was just fact!"

"Weird. I've never heard of that." However, Samantha could see why some witches would choose to not believe in good and evil. Some people were content being a bit ignorant to live happy lives. If it's what they needed to do to keep them going,

Samantha was not going to judge.

"I know," Danielle said. "But there's no way to convince them, really. I have nothing to show them otherwise. Not that witches have ever needed proof to believe anything before."

"That's true." The dog picked the fire hydrant across the street to lift his leg to. The couple waited until he was finished before continuing out of sight.

"One woman even slammed the door in my face. From the smell of her house, she was either cloaking it completely from sight or smoking something. I'm really not sure which."

Samantha hadn't realized Danielle was making house calls. Just another way that she felt like she wasn't pulling her weight in this partnership. Would those witches in California be more likely to listen to her if she was face-to-face? Probably, but getting there would require magic and timing. Not to mention that Steven would never like the idea.

"Well, the biggest thing is that we've identified three out of the five branches," Samantha said. "That's huge for such a short time."

"Yeah." Danielle paused, then added, "That actually worries me a little."

"Why?"

"If they're supposed to be so private, how was it so easy for us to find them?"

Shoot. Samantha hadn't thought of it that way. "Maybe because we know what we're looking for?" Her voice didn't indicate confidence in that idea.

"Maybe…I'm just leery about this. I mean, I still have no idea how to kill Toxanna; how am I supposed to take out four other people who are just as strong as she is?"

"With help." *That* was something Samantha *could* help with.

"I can't ask you to do that."

"You're not. I'm offering. As soon as we figure out what the Pentad is up to, we can focus on taking out each branch member, starting with Toxanna." Once they got to that point, Samantha would tell Kathy about all of this. Although, she didn't know exactly how that conversation would go. Not after hiding it from her for so long.

"Thanks," Danielle said.

"So you think Toxanna is the water branch then?"

"I guess so. It's hard to tell because I'm so close to her. I know her too well, so it's hard for me to see the bigger picture, you know?" Danielle sighed. "But there is a lot of time that I can't account for where she was. Was she just hiding in the corner and planning her next move on my family, or was she gathering more power so that she can kill us in one shot?"

"I don't know."

Samantha waited for Danielle to respond, but she could tell her new friend was lost in her own thoughts and worries about her family. While Samantha and Kathy regularly faced their own share of evil, they hadn't even come close to the pain and heartbreak that Danielle had experienced.

"I guess we just have to move forward with the mindset that Toxanna is working with the Pentad," Samantha said. "So now how do we defeat her?"

"I don't know!" Danielle bellowed, frustrated. She let out a sigh to calm herself. "Just do me a favor: write a spell in your magic book to kill her. Even if it doesn't work, it'll be better than nothing. Hopefully you won't ever have to use it."

"Sure, yeah," Samantha said calmly. Spells were Kathy's area of expertise, but since this was still Samantha's solo mission, she'd have to come up with one on her own. "It's going to be hard because I don't know her as well as you do, but I'll see what I can come up with."

"Okay, thanks. I'm just glad that you haven't added any major threats to you and your sister with this."

Samantha laughed. "We still have our fair share of magical nuisances, but nothing major lately." She tapped on the wooden frame of the chair. "Knock on wood!"

CHAPTER 5

- FEBRUARY 6, 1989 -
MONDAY

The Pentad?" the woman behind the counter asked. Her forehead scrunched in confusion as she stared at Samantha.

"Yes. They're a coven made up of very powerful magic practitioners. Their powers are related to the five magical elements."

"Like elementals?"

"Um…" Samantha pursed her lips, considering. "Not quite, but similar, I guess."

The woman shook her head. "I haven't heard anything like that. I'm, um…nonmagical?" She looked to Samantha to confirm she had the word right.

Samantha nodded. "Okay, but you work in an occult shop.

Surely you've heard *something*."

She was getting desperate. Guilty that she wasn't contributing as much to this partnership as Danielle was, Samantha decided to make use of her own connections: talking to the occult shops in Erie. There were only two, which was significant for the relatively small size of their city. Talia and Cassandra at Mystic Treasures hadn't heard anything, but they agreed to keep their ears perked for any whispers they might hear, whether in their shop or spiritually.

This woman, Margaret, was being frustratingly obtuse, in Samantha's opinion. The Apothecary leaned more into the novelty aspect of the occult business—likely to distract from its true demographic target—but even a lowly clerk had to have some kind of insight into why customers were there and what they chitchatted about.

Margaret shook her head again. "I'm sorry, ma'am. I haven't heard anything about this…pentacle."

"Pentad," Samantha corrected.

"Whatever. Is there something in the shop I can help you with? We recently got these precious gems in, which are incredibly pretty. And the labels claim they help with healing and focus. How fun!"

Samantha offered a polite smile and turned toward the door. "No thanks. I'm all set."

"Oh okay. Well, I hope to see you in here again! It was nice chatting with you."

"You too," Samantha muttered as she pushed the door open and stepped out into the parking lot in front of the building. She squinted in the harsh winter sun. The light reflected off the fallen snow and even blinded her as she diverted her eyes to the pavement, which had been dyed white from an excess of salt.

This had been a waste of time and only served to further diminish her hope that she could actually help Danielle with the Pentad. Or worse, that the Pentad would catch on that she was asking questions and corner her or Kathy before they had come up with a game plan.

Just another thing to vent to Danielle about later when she called. Kathy was working and Steven was going to have dinner with his parents, so she would have the house to herself.

"Excuse me?" a woman called as Samantha was just about to step into her car. The woman had beautiful long hair, dark features, and she wore a leather jacket pulled tightly across her body. Even in the February cold, she looked stylish and attractive.

"Oh, hello." Samantha was in the business attire she wore to the office, since she made this useless excursion on her lunch break. Her stomach growled, signaling part of the reason for her foul mood.

Probably should've just stayed at the office and opted for food instead.

"I heard you talking…" the woman said quietly.

Samantha stepped closer and pushed behind her ear. "I'm sorry, what?"

The roar of vehicles on West 26th Street behind them made casual conversation nearly impossible. After the street had been converted to a four lane highway, the whole area had been transformed to compete with the suburban development style being built on the edge of the city. It was an effort to make the area more marketable to suburbanites, but what it ended up doing was destroying the vibrancy of the neighborhood.

The woman extended her hand and leaned in as Samantha shook it. "My name's Olivia. I heard you talking inside."

Samantha stiffened. "Oh?"

"How did you hear about the supergroup?"

"Um…from other witches." Samantha wasn't sure if her fear had materialized. Maybe this woman was someone who was a member of the Pentad. Or closely connected with them.

Maybe it was a good thing there was an overbuilt road behind them. Not that anyone would stop and actually get out of their car. In Samantha's experience, pedestrians became invisible to people behind the wheel.

"What witches?"

"Are you part of the Pentad?" Samantha asked pointedly.

Olivia stepped back and shook her head. "Uh…"

Quickly, before she was completely scared away, Samantha dove into Olivia's mind. She'd been getting better at this new power. The thoughts at the forefront were easier to read. And it was obvious that Samantha's interrogation method needed improving.

Does she know about me? Olivia's voice said in Samantha's head. *About how I was asked me to be a part of the Pentad?*

Samantha wondered who would've asked her and how they'd chosen Olivia, but she sensed more thoughts on her mind and she needed to stall to give her time to read them.

"I'm sorry." Samantha chanced a half-step forward, trying to keep in close contact with Olivia so she could continue to tap into her mind. "That was out of line. I was just curious. I'm Samantha, by the way. I don't think I properly introduced myself."

"Do you know about the Pentad?" Olivia asked. *Is she one of them? Would she be my sister if I joined?* "Oh, honey, joining a demonic coven like this is not going to be like having a family."

It wasn't until Samantha saw Olivia's horrified expression on her face that she realized she screwed up, responding to Olivia's thoughts instead of her words.

Olivia began to back away, but Samantha grabbed ahold of her arm.

"Let me go," she warned.

"Hear me out," Samantha said. "The Pentad is bad news. You need to carefully disentangle yourself from them and move on. They're not going to make good on any of the promises they offered you."

"And I should believe you? You're the one hunting them down."

"To stop them! Olivia, the beings in this coven are dangerous. And they want to train you to be too."

She yanked her arm away from Samantha's grasp. "And I'm supposed to believe someone who read my mind? How do I know you're not just manipulating me?"

"Olivia, no. I'm being sincere! I'm trying to help!"

"Leave me alone or I'm calling the police."

Without waiting for a reply, she turned and rushed off to her own car. Samantha took a few steps to try to catch her, but knew it was a lost cause. She watched helplessly as Olivia backed out of her parking spot and swerved onto the street, quickly merging into traffic.

Way to go, Sam, she thought to herself. *You blew the only lead you had in Erie.*

CHAPTER 6

Samantha raced back to the Apothecary after work, hoping to catch Margaret—or another worker—before they closed up shop for the day. She was glad to see the OPEN sign still shone in the window.

"Welcome to the Apothecary—oh! Hello again!" Margaret smiled brightly when she recognized Samantha. She had a small cart of items to stock on the shelves, which she pulled behind her.

"Oh good, you do remember me."

"Of course!"

"Do you also remember the woman I was talking to out in the parking lot when I left this afternoon?"

Margaret made a face. "Dark hair? Very pretty?"

"Yes! Her name's Olivia and I need to get in touch with her. I never got her phone number—or better yet, her address."

Margaret's smile faltered. "Well…that's not usually information we give out about customers."

"Please, it's really important." Samantha had tried looking in the phone book while she was at work, but since she didn't know Olivia's last name, it was an impossible search.

"What is the emergency?"

"Remember the supergroup I was asking about earlier? I think they might be after her." Margaret adjusted a set of decorative bowls on the shelf. "Next time she comes in I could—"

"Next time isn't good enough!" Samantha blurted. She saw the surprised look on Margaret's face at the outburst, then offered, "Sorry. Um…why don't I look around and browse for a bit? I need to cool down before I can get behind the wheel again."

Margaret nodded. "Of course. Take your time. We're open until six."

Samantha checked her watch. Just about five-thirty. She examined the set of bowls Margaret was just fussing over. Then she moved to the trinkets against the wall. It was her way of disarming Margaret so that she could probe her mind.

And it worked. Margaret pushed the cart with overstock to the side and shuffled back behind the counter. She turned to the magazine left open on the counter and flipped through it casually.

Inching closer, Samantha extended her mind specialty out toward Margaret and successfully probed her thoughts. Pushing past her surface thoughts, she dug deeper into her memory, straining at the effort. This was some of the most deliberate use of this new extension of her power and she didn't want to overextend herself.

Finally, as Samantha felt herself flush with heat from the effort, she located the part in Margaret's mind where she kept information on Olivia. A list of herbs were all that Samantha could read, along with the usual time of day that Olivia arrived, and a memory of Olivia denying Margaret's offer to order ingredients they were missing, opting instead to come back another time.

Pulling out of her thoughts, Samantha wiped away the sweat from her brow. She was frustrated that Margaret truly didn't know anything. And if Olivia never ordered anything from the shop, then there was probably no record of her address anywhere at the Apothecary.

Samantha stepped to the counter and asked for some herbs she'd been meaning to restock. It was her effort not to make Margaret more suspicious of her. Besides, she needed the herbs anyway.

As she drove home, she tried to think of other ways to track down Olivia. They had only met for a brief moment. Nothing long enough to make a lasting impression. And it's not like Samantha had anything of Olivia's to use with a location ritual. She was stuck.

When she finally pulled into her driveway, she was surprised to see Steven's car parked in front of her. She walked around to the front door and let herself in, where the lights in the foyer were on.

"Honey?" she called through the house.

"Back here!" he said from the kitchen.

She kicked off her heels and walked barefoot across the hardwood and into the kitchen. "What are you doing home? I thought you were supposed to have dinner with your parents?"

Steven was standing at the stove with a pot of pasta boiling. He wore an apron that Samantha had bought him as a birthday present as a joke. Now that they were married, he insisted on using it to develop his domesticated side.

"Grandpa Jack fell today and they went over there to check on him." Steven gave her a sideways hug and a quick peck before returning to the stove.

"Is he okay?" Samantha settled in at the kitchen island.

"I think so. But he doesn't like the fuss, you know? So I thought it was better if I rescheduled with my parents. They are already more company than he wants in a situation like this. And my dad would call if anything turned serious."

"Well, I hope he's okay."

"Me too. What about you? You're home late. Out cruising the bars, looking for a new husband already?" He grinned.

"Please, managing one is hard enough."

"I'm sorry, I'm pretty sure *I'm* the one standing at the stove while you're sitting on your ass."

She laughed. "True. I'm trying to track down this witch who has been approached by the Pentad to join."

"The Pentad is this supergroup that you've been tracking despite my better judgement?"

"Yeah. I ran into her at the Apothecary on my lunch."

"What were you doing out there on your lunch?" He waved the steam away from the ladle as he taste-tested a particular noodle.

"I thought maybe I could ask around about the Pentad or anyone connected. See if anyone knew anything."

Steven gave her a look.

"Nothing bad happened!" she pleaded.

"Is that where you met this woman?"

"She overheard me and caught up with me in the parking lot."

"Who else might've overheard you?"

"You know, this is part of the reason why I haven't told Kathy about all of this," Samantha said. "I don't need the lecture."

Steven put up his hands in surrender. "I'm just saying. I want you to be careful."

"I am."

"So what did you do when she told you that she was asked to join?"

She stretched out across the island and buried her face in her arms. "Well…she didn't exactly *tell* me."

"You read her mind?"

She sprang upright. "It was on the tip of her tongue anyway!"

"And I'm guessing you freaked her out."

"Well, I mean…" She shrugged.

"So now what?"

"Now I want to find her, apologize for scaring her, and try to get some answers about who approached her so Danielle and I can track them down."

Steven switched off the burner and reached for a set of potholders. "You understand how crazy you are, right? You're literally tracking down trouble."

Samantha waved it off. "I was trying to come up with ways I could locate her. I thought maybe I could go to the police and use my persuasion on them to run a check into her and have them track her down for me."

"Remember that thing you said before that was crazy? You just topped that."

She glared at him. "I was hoping you'd be supportive."

He finished pouring the pasta into the strainer in the sink and returned the pot to the stove. "Sam, think about it: persuading the police department with magic would be crossing a major ethical line."

"But I don't know how else to find her!"

Steven added sauce to the pot and turned the burner to simmer. "You're a smart witch. You'll figure out another way—a *legal* way—to track her down. And you'll be smart enough to stop when it starts to get dangerous."

Samantha made a face. "I suppose I could go back to the Apothecary and use my persuasion on Margaret. See if she can tell me who might know where Olivia lives."

"There you go!"

"I tried probing her mind earlier, but she didn't have any record of Olivia's address. Not that I could find, at least."

Steven added in the pasta to the sauce. "So when you go into people's heads, are memories stored in like a large storage facility with a lot of file cabinets, or…how does that work?"

"It's hard to explain, but everything's compartmentalized in a way, yes."

He stirred the pasta and the sauce, then turned off the burner. "Interesting."

Samantha scooted off the stool and helped him gather plates and silverware. "Thanks for making dinner."

"Of course." He grabbed a bottle of wine from the rack and screwed in the corkscrew. "Just try not to think about this supergroup too much. I want you to relax tonight. It is just the two of us, after all." He popped the cork on the bottle and reached for two wine glasses.

She grinned. "Oh? Did you have some ideas for after dinner?"

"I just want to make the most of our quiet evenings together." He offered her a glass of wine and raised his. They clinked. "To you and me, babe."

CHAPTER 7

So other than this business with this supergroup that you keep sticking your nose into, how's life?" Steven took a bite of food, waiting Samantha's reply.

They were seated in the dining room with the lights from the chandelier dimmed to set the mood, but not too low that they couldn't see. They had made *that* mistake the first time they had a dinner date at home.

"Good," Samantha said after a sip of wine. "Work's good. We're gearing up for tax season, which is why Mr. Marsden sent me to that conference in Saratoga. It's my first tax-season as a CPA, so he wants to make sure I'm prepared."

"Overworked and underpaid, in my opinion." Steven knew what it was like during tax season since he worked for a tax firm as well. Different types of accounts, but still just as crazy each spring. "Which is why I think it's important to make the most of our time alone, before the storm begins to swirl in."

Samantha skewered the pasta in her dish. "The accounts are already coming in. My workload has already started picking up."

"And that makes you want to hunt down trouble?" She shot him a look and he added, "Sorry. It just came out."

"Is this going to be a problem? Me being a witch when I'm also your wife?"

"I just want you to be careful."

"I am careful, but things happen sometimes. Things that sometimes put me in a dangerous situation."

He stared at the wineglass in his hand and sighed heavily. "You know I'm worried, but it's more than that. I know your priorities have to shift away from us sometimes, but…"

"But what?" she prompted after the end of his sentence never came.

"Never mind." He shook his head and took a big sip from his own glass.

"No, tell me. We're alone. We're talking. We're being honest. It's good to start a marriage on honesty. I want ours to be successful. So let's talk. Even if it's uncomfortable." Another sigh. "Are you even thinking about kids for us?"

Samantha's gaze dropped to her plate. This was the conversation they were having again. She'd been able to successfully dodge it on the honeymoon, but now there was no excuse. And the vision she got with Danielle was inconclusive in answering her question about any potential children. It did, however, remind her that any children she would have would be witches, just like her.

"Being a witch, I'm used to a certain level of danger," she said. "I just…don't know if I'd be comfortable with that same level of danger with children around."

He nodded slowly. "I suppose this is probably a discussion we should've had *before* the wedding."

Her eyes snapped up to his. "Are you saying you wouldn't have married me if you knew I wasn't sure about kids?"

"No, that's not what I'm saying, but—kids are important to me, Sam. I always thought we'd have them."

"I'm not saying no."

"But you're saying probably not."

"I'm just saying I'm nervous."

"I'm nervous too! Even without you being a witch. What if I screw it up? What if they fall and get hurt? What if tax season becomes a problem and I'm never home because of it? Or you? What if our marriage gets strained because of the added pressure? These are the things *I* worry about."

Samantha smiled at her husband and reached across the table. She loved it when he thought of the future. Of their little family. And if he was willing to face his fears about Samantha being a witch, she could face some of hers about children. They both had the same goal, after all: to be a family.

"I love it that that's what you think about." She squeezed his hand. "And I'm sorry if it seemed like I was being dismissive of that. I'm not saying I don't want kids, but I'm more nervous about it than you are because of everything else from my world…complicating things. But I do know you're going to be a great dad."

"So what does that mean? Do you want to start trying?"

Samantha took a big gulp of her wine. "I don't think I'm quite ready for *that* yet. I'm happy just being your wife for now. Maybe in a year we can talk about it again. And if it happens before that, then it happens. If not, we can talk about trying after our anniversary."

He smiled. "Deal."

"I mean, we *just* got married. Not even a month ago."

"I know, but I'm anxious. And all this free time we've had with the house to ourselves is…enticing."

"And you want to steal that free time away by having kids?"

"We're just going to practice!"

She laughed, then glanced at their plates. They were about halfway done. And it was just pasta. Something that could easily be reheated in the microwave.

"Okay then." She stood and came around the table to reach for his hand. "Let's enjoy the house to ourselves then."

"Really?" He rose and stumbled along with her toward

the stairs. "Right now? We're not even done eating."

"The food can wait."

Laughing, they hurried up the stairs to the bedroom.

CHAPTER 8

- FEBRUARY 7, 1989 -
TUESDAY

The bell above the door at the Apothecary jingled as Samantha stepped through after a long day of work at the office. Her workload had already begun building with incoming clients for annual tax returns, on top of their usual accounts. To make it worse, Mr. Marsden said that an audit was looming soon, which meant even more work, probably well into the summer, if not the fall.

"Hello again!" Margaret said with a smile. "Here for more herbs?"

Samantha shook her head. "Actually, I wanted to ask if I could be of any help."

"Oh?"

"I'm considering starting my own little side business selling herbs from my garden and I was wondering if I could get a quick tutorial on how you guys do your ordering?" She laced her words with persuasion, which was a skill she had long mastered.

"I suppose that would be okay." Margaret ushered Samantha around to the other side of the counter as she pulled out an order book. "All of our orders are recorded here. And we indicate their name, their phone number, what they ordered, of course. We also put in the vendor number of who we need to contact to order it."

Samantha followed where Margaret pointed to another large notebook under the counter.

"We have a whole separate book with vendors that we keep updated," Margaret said. "When you're on the phone with a customer, it's better to just get what they want and then find the vendor later. If you have to call them back with updated shipping times, then that's that, but at least they're not waiting while you're sorting through these books."

"You don't collect their address?" Samantha asked.

"We do if they would rather have their items shipped directly to them. A lot of our customers prefer to stop in. It's so convenient since they added the parking lot up front."

Convenient until a flashier, newer store is built further out from town, Samantha thought. *Or someone gets hit by a car flying off the road.*

"How many other people work here?"

"There's four of us, including the owner. I usually work the evening shifts, then we have Laurie who does the weekends, and Debbie does week days. And, of course, the owner. But I've been filling in a lot since Debbie's been on vacation. She went down to Florida and…"

Margaret rambled on, but Samantha stopped listening.

Samantha had hoped that there were more people working here. Since she worked all day, she had only been able to investigate Margaret's mind, which told her that Olivia hadn't ordered anything *from her*. But perhaps she had ordered something—and had it delivered to her home—from one of the other girls working.

"I think you should probably check on those herbs over there." Samantha pointed across the shop to the display by the window. "They look a little droopy. I'm going to check out this book more."

"Oh okay!" Aided by Samantha's persuasion power, Margaret set off to do what Samantha had suggested without a second thought otherwise.

In her absence, Samantha flipped through the order book, searching for Olivia's name. Through pages and pages, she briefly glanced up at Margaret, who was so perfectly fussing with her array of plants that she was oblivious to Samantha's frantic search.

Finally, toward the front of the book, Samantha spotted Olivia's name, alongside an address. She didn't immediately recognize the area, but she transcribed the address on a scrap piece of paper anyway. Stuffing it in her pocket, she buttoned up her coat and stepped to the door.

"Thanks for your help, Margaret," she said. "I really appreciate it."

"Anytime, dear. Have a great day! And good luck with your business!"

Back in the nighttime cold, Samantha got behind the wheel and merged back into the speeding traffic that felt more like a raceway than a street.

Olivia lived at Grandview Manor. Samantha guessed that it was an apartment. The street address was on Davison Avenue, which didn't ring any bells with Samantha. She was currently on 26th Street and it ran through most of the city. So she stuck to the right lane and watched for street signs, hoping to catch a glimpse of Davison as she drove on and on.

Over at the city's industrial area, where the main train routes used to come through from the north, 26th Street hooked left toward the lake. Samantha turned right onto Elm, hoping to check for more streets up on 28th Street, which also extended through most of the city. At this point, her optimism had slowly faded. But, if she couldn't find it tonight, she could go back home, check a map, and go right to Olivia's tomorrow.

That was her last resort.

As soon as she was on 28th Street, she checked the street signs: Tuttle, Burns, Gloth, New, and…Davison!

Hitting her turn signal, she took a right onto the street and hoped the apartment complex was easy to spot.

She passed all the numbered streets, crossing over into more suburban territory with wider lots, ranch-style houses that all looked the same, and more box stores and gas stations.

Tucked behind a large oak tree in front of a tiny gray house, Samantha caught sight of the red sign that said, "Grandview Manor." She swung in, pulled into the first parking spot she could find, and marched to the front door.

She managed to catch it just as another resident was leaving, allowing her access without having to persuade someone to let her in. Skipping the elevator and going right to the stairs, she climbed up to the third floor to find 313. It was halfway down the hallway on the right.

With her fist raised to knock, Samantha heard yelps and hissing. She listened closely, but the noises didn't sound anything like a cat or anything else that might be coming from inside the apartment. With the thought of the Pentad on her mind, Samantha tried the door and was surprised to find it unlocked.

She stepped right into chaos.

Olivia stood among a swarm of imps, tiny devil-like creatures that flew around her face like gnats. The walls were bare, likely stripped of the few decorations from the use of magic, which was evident by the broken glass on the floor and the utter disarray of everything else in the small apartment.

Swinging her arms around, Olivia conjured a gust of wind and sent the imps slamming against the wall like a series of shot-puts.

"Woah," Samantha let slip, which drew Olivia's attention.

It was enough distraction for the imps to recover, picking up their little bodies from the floor and racing after Olivia in another effort to attack.

This time, Samantha was faster. She tapped into her telepathy, which she had been working on a lot lately, and pushed her command into the small minds of the imps: "Stop and retreat!"

The effort left her weak and she leaned on the wall for support, but still, the imps listened and each disappeared in a quick puff of smoke.

Samantha grinned at having been successful with her new power, but turned serious when she looked at the venomous glare coming from Olivia.

"What the hell are *you* doing here?"

CHAPTER 9

nd how did you find me?" Olivia added.

Samantha decided not to reveal how she manipulated Margaret with her power. "I just want to talk."

"You want to convince me not to join the Pentad."

"Well…yes," Samantha admitted. "But I don't think you quite understand why. It's a bad idea, Olivia. It will be the end of you."

"Get out of here!" she bellowed, extending her arm toward the door behind Samantha. "You don't know me. I can make my own decisions!"

"Think about it, Olivia." Samantha pushed her persuasion power through her words. "They're making all of these promises to get you to join, maybe they'll even come through on some of them, but then they'll start asking you to do a favor to benefit the group even if it hurts you, then another. Next thing you know, you have a role to fill for them that has nothing to do with the reasons you joined them to begin with."

The magic was taking effect. Olivia paused, her face contorting in confusion.

"They're using you," Samantha went on. "They just want your power. Want your specialty to fill a void in the magical makeup of their group. They're preying on your desire to have a family. They don't—"

Suddenly, Olivia shook her head. "My desire to have a family? I've never said that out loud. You got that idea when you picked my brain!"

Samantha cursed herself for screwing up something that she thought she had mastered. The elevation of her powers made everything more complicated. Not to mention, she was still weakened from controlling the imps.

Olivia backed away, extending her hand out toward Samantha in warning. "Stay away from me or I'll use *my* power."

"No, wait. I'm trying to help you." Samantha took a step forward, but Olivia sent a forceful gust of wind at her, which caused her to fly back against the wall.

Taking advantage of the moment, Olivia grabbed her

purse and started to the door. "I told you I can take care of myself. Leave me alone."

From the floor, Samantha watched as Olivia stormed out of the apartment.

CHAPTER 10

Samantha took a sip of her Pepsi from the booth in the corner of the Red Fox Inn bar. The name indicated the place was more than a dive, but it was just a ruse. Maybe once upon a time there had been rooms for rent above the bar, but Samantha very much doubted there was any level of hospitality offered beyond the purchase of an adult beverage.

The booth she sat in had been ripped and mended with duct tape, so it wasn't the most comfortable seat in the place. But it still allowed her the clearest vantage point to the door and to Olivia behind the bar.

After Olivia had stormed out of the apartment, Samantha followed and managed to get into her car just as Olivia was leaving the parking lot of Grandview Manor. When she had turned onto 38th Street, she thought she lost Olivia in the traffic. Luckily, the bar was just around the corner from the apartment so Samantha had caught up to Olivia pulling into the bar while she was still sitting at the stoplight.

When Samantha had walked in, though, Olivia shot her a dirty look but otherwise ignored her. She was, after all, at work and had customers to tend to.

The bar was slow, especially with it being a Wednesday evening. There were the obvious regulars who called Olivia by name—which was better than "honey," "sweetie," or more vulgar names Samantha knew no woman appreciated. Still, she watched as Olivia flirted with all the guys—despite what they called her—which resulted in bigger bills left on the bar top after they had had their fill.

For the first time since she arrived an hour ago, Samantha moved from her seat to squeeze into the phone booth in the corner. She pulled the privacy door closed, but the country twang playing from the speakers was still pretty loud in the booth.

After sliding in the right amount of coins, she dialed the house and was glad Steven was the one who answered.

"Hey honey, it's me," she said.

"Sam? Where are you?"

"At a bar on 38th."

"Um…"

"I found Olivia and followed her here. She's the bartender."

"I thought you were going to talk to her?"

Samantha looked over her shoulder to make sure Olivia was still serving and not running. "I tried. She didn't want to listen."

"So what's your plan then?"

"I figured I'd watch to make sure she doesn't try to join the Pentad."

"You're going to follow her for the rest of her life?"

"Of course not. Just until…I don't know."

"I don't like this, Sam."

"I know," she said, then changed the subject. "Where's Kathy?"

He sighed, obviously not thrilled that she hadn't agreed to come home. "She left a little while ago to head to the library. I guess she's got a group project or something and they're meeting about it."

"Did she ask where I was?"

"I don't even think she noticed you weren't home."

"Good. Don't tell her. Now that she's started classes again and she's trying to work as many hours as possible at the store, she has enough on her plate."

"And you don't?"

"I can handle it."

His silence told her he disagreed.

"She's already done a lot for me—for us—with our wedding a couple weeks ago," Samantha added. "I don't want to burden her anymore."

"But I don't want you to get hurt in the meantime. Not with you chasing down other witches who are involved with bad people."

"If it comes to it, then I guess you can tell her. But I'd rather you didn't."

"And what do you want me to say if she *does* ask?"

Samantha looked over at Olivia. The two locked eyes, sizing each other up. Both witches were ready to wait the other out. It was a matter of wills. "Just…tell her that I'm working late."

CHAPTER 11

It had been a long time since Samantha had stayed up past midnight. Probably not since Kathy had dragged her to a party or some other nocturnal outing. The far side of two AM didn't feel any better than it sounded, and Samantha knew she was going to kick herself for staying up so late when she had to be at work in seven hours.

The last of the customers had left after last call. Other than the news playing on the TV above the bar, the place was quiet. Olivia busied herself with restocking the drinks under the bar and using a rag to clean the bar top.

She disappeared in the back and Samantha wondered if she was going to turn off the lights and leave her there, but she returned shortly after with a mop and a bucket to clean up the salt and slush near the door that had been tracked in from the parking lot.

After she finished swabbing up the mess, she turned to Samantha, put a hand on her hip, and abruptly asked, "So how long are you going to be following me? Because, I gotta say, it's Day One and it's already creepy."

Samantha swung her feet out of the booth to stand. She tucked her hair behind her ears and was about to cross her arms to craft a response to Olivia's question when suddenly there were three men surrounding them that appeared in the blink of an eye. Both women jumped at the sight of the tattooed newcomers. They were clad in dark clothing with sinister looks. One sported a thick beard, another looked as if his shoulders were about to bust the seams of his jacket, and the third had a persistent scowl. One-by-one, they each summoned a ball of fire in their palms.

"Take cover!" Samatha shouted. She dove behind the bar for protection.

Olivia raised her arms up, as if in a last-ditch effort to shield her face, but a sudden gust of wind erupted from her hands, sending the men tumbling backward.

Samantha watched from behind the bar, her groggy mind trying to piece together where these men had come from and why they were here. Clearly, they were demonic, but what did they want with her or Olivia?

And, hopefully, Steven's fears wouldn't come true.

Then it hit her: Olivia had already been asked to join the Pentad, which would make that coven much stronger. And if there was one thing Samantha knew about the demonic world, it was that they didn't like when one group outranked the other and disturbed the distorted order they had grown accustomed to.

These men—demons, likely—were trying to kill Olivia before she could join the Pentad and become even more powerful. Essentially, they wanted the same thing Samantha wanted, except Samantha wasn't going to kill Olivia for it.

Meanwhile, Olivia managed to hold her own against the attack, fending off fireballs with her control over the wind. Still, there were three of them and only one of Olivia. When a fireball went rogue and shattered the bottles of liquor stacked against the wall behind the bar, Samantha knew she needed to step up and help the witch out.

Getting to her feet, Samantha darted behind Olivia for protection as she fended off attacks from the encroaching demons.

"What are you *doing*?" Olivia murmured through gritted teeth.

"Trying to help," Samantha said. "I'm going to try to do what I did with the imps and take control of their minds. I'm exhausted, but I think I'll buy you enough time to get out of here. Don't go home. Go stay with a friend or somewhere where they can't find you."

"And what about you?"

Samantha smiled, glad that Olivia still had a good heart to worry about a total stranger. A stranger who was, admittedly, annoying her by hovering. Obviously, rightfully so.

"They're not after me," Samantha said. "They'll disappear once they realize you're gone." She hoped that was true. There really was no Plan B. "Ready?"

Olivia nodded.

Samantha counted down from three, then extended her hands outward toward the men, trying to probe all three of them at once. Besides the imps, she had never penetrated the minds of more than one person at once. Until recently, she hadn't been able to push into the mind of anyone by will. The effort quickly drained what little energy she had left.

But it worked.

The three men stood, frozen in their spot, unable to move under Samantha's control. Their fireballs had been extinguished, their limbs frozen in place. The only command she was sending to them was a simple one: stop. All three looked at Samantha with venomous eyes.

Maybe they *would* go after Samantha once Olivia escaped.

With the demons under the mind control, Olivia took a cautious step forward, then another. She looked back at Samantha, who wanted to tell her to run, but was afraid the effort would cause her control to slip, leaving them both vulnerable.

Olivia seemed to pick up on that. Quietly, she said, "Thank you," and took another step toward the door, crossing between two of the demons. Both men, glared at her, still unable to move.

Samantha, however, was growing weaker. Her fatigue building with each passing second and she didn't know how much longer she could hold—

The man with the beard moved, snatching Olivia's arm just before she was able to grab ahold of the door. She screamed and squirmed, but he held tight.

The other man followed, with Samantha's control crumbling completely, just as she slumped to the floor in exhaustion.

Helplessly, Samantha watched as Olivia's other arm was restrained by the second man. The third approached her and together, all four of them disappeared in the blink of an eye.

And Samantha had no idea where.

CHAPTER 12

Admittedly, Samantha wasn't being quiet as she fumbled in the kitchen to slap together a location ritual. Before she left the bar, she grabbed Olivia's car keys and brought them home with her to use in the ritual. It was the most personal item of Olivia's that she could find.

Now that it was just about three in the morning, sleep was the farthest thing from Samantha's mind. She could only think about finding Olivia and saving her before those demons got to her—or worse.

"Would you take it easy?" Steven stepped into the kitchen in his bathrobe. "You woke me up. I'm surprised you didn't wake up Kathy too."

"She's home?" Samantha kept her focus on the lighter as

she tried to ignite the four yellow candles surrounding the bowl of water. It flickered several times, but no flame lasted long enough to catch the wick. She tossed it in the sink with a loud clang and opened the junk drawer for another one. "I thought we had a lighter in here!"

"Sam, what's going on? You're scaring me."

"They took her."

"Who? Kathy's upstairs, last I checked."

"Not her. Olivia."

"Where?"

"I don't know!" She grabbed a handful of the contents of the drawer and piled it on the counter. Markers, paper clips, flashlights, and other errant objects scattered across the countertop, some rolling off the edge to the floor.

Steven came around and put his hands on Samantha's to slow her down. "Take a breath and relax for half a second."

"If they hurt her—"

"Tearing apart the house is not going to save her any faster."

Samantha took a deep breath, trying to push away the guilt she felt for not being able to save her. If Olivia had continued to fend them off, maybe Samantha could've come up with another plan for both of them to escape. Or maybe she should've used her persuasion on all three men to convince them to leave, instead of being cocky and trying to use her new power.

"I need to find her," she said in a wavering voice. Pulling away from her husband, she snatched up a new lighter and lit the four candles.

Despite the audible huff coming from Steven, she placed Olivia's keys in front of the bowl of water and recited:

I call on the strength of my power,
show Olivia's face in the water.

The water began to ripple, then the reflection changed from Samantha's face to Olivia. Through the bowl, Samantha could see Olivia clear as day. She was tied to a chair with the three men standing cross-armed around her. So she wasn't hurt. Not yet, at least.

But where was she?

Samantha tried to examine Olivia's surroundings in the murky water. It was dark, but she noticed the unkempt room. Curtains pulled away from the windows, couch cushions tossed on the floor, the stuffing littering the carpet.

They were at Olivia's apartment. Which meant that they had known where she was all along. They would've struck whether Samantha was there or not. That realization didn't help Samantha feel any better.

"So?" Steven asked.

"I know where she is." Samantha blew out the candles, snatched up Olivia's keys, and then went to her purse for her own keys.

"You're going *now*?"

"She's in danger, Steve!"

"Then I'm coming with you."

She looked him up and down. "Like hell you are!"

"Well, you're not going alone. Would you rather I wake up Kathy and tell her?"

Samantha clenched her fists around both sets of keys. It was a wonder Kathy was still oblivious to this whole mess. But telling her now would only lead to more questions, more explanations, more time that Olivia might not have.

"Sam, I'm not going to lose my wife right after I married her," Steven said. "Not when you just need to slow down a bit."

She looked at the clock: 3:13. It had been almost forty-five minutes since they had been first attacked. There was no telling how much more time Olivia had, which meant Samantha needed to get to her at all costs.

"Fine. Go put on pants. I'm going to stock up on potions, just in case."

Just in case my magic fails me again, she thought to herself.

"But make it quick. I'm not waiting."

CHAPTER 13

Samantha and Steven pulled into the parking lot of Grandview Manor just after 3:30 in the morning. The lot was full, dimly lit by two lights in the center of the parking lot.

Near the entrance, there were a group of people smoking, eyeing up Samantha's car as she pulled in. They looked like they were up to no good, but Samantha didn't care. She needed to get to Olivia before her situation turned worse.

"Stay here," Samantha said to Steven as she slung a satchel bag over her shoulder. It was full of potions she had pulled from the cabinet back at the house. Ones she had made for emergency situations.

"Sam—" he began to protest, but she cut him off.

"*Don't* push me on this, Steven." She slammed the car door to prove her point and walked up to the main entrance, which was right next to the group of smokers. She frowned when the locked door gave resistance.

"You ain't from around here, are you?" one of the smokers asked her.

The rest of the group chuckled.

"What's the password, sweetheart?" another man asked around the cigarette hanging from his lip.

Samantha didn't have time to waste playing prey to a bunch of nocturnal thugs, so she pushed her persuasion out heavily with her words.

"Just leave me alone and open the door for me." She added a sarcastic, "Please."

Sure, she had Olivia's keys with her, but she didn't have time to fumble around and guess at which one opened the door to the building. Upstairs, she could probably figure out the apartment key if she needed to.

The smoker closest to the door pulled a key from his pocket, opened the door, and held it for her to pass through.

"Thanks," she said over her shoulder as she darted into the lackluster lobby. A fluorescent light flickered just above the door, while the others shed a blindingly white light that erased any sense of homeliness.

Skipping the elevator, she went right for the stairs, taking them two at a time up to the third floor. She raced down the hall to apartment 313.

Outside Olivia's door, she heard muffled screams coming from a woman. After finding the only key that looked like a door key, she slid it into the slot, swung open the door, and charged inside.

Just like she saw in the water bowl back at the house, Olivia was strapped to a chair. Only this time, the demons were each taking turns holding fireballs to her skin. Olivia screamed with each turn of torture. All up and down her arms were red, angry burns.

"Hey!" Samantha called out. She pulled a vial from her satchel bag and lobbed it at the floor, near the feet of the demons. Each of the demons caught fire—first just their clothing, then quickly spreading to the rest of their body.

Seeing the effects of the potion, Samantha remembered brewing it. She had designed it to reverse the effects of an enemy's magic, making them feel what they had intended for others.

Unlike Olivia, though, the demons weren't strong enough to handle the heat. Flame consumed them and they each let out their own screams until one-by-one they disintegrated into a pile of ash on the floor.

Rushing to Olivia's side, Samantha tried to loosen the phone wire on her left wrist that was binding her to the chair. She didn't make much progress before she felt something smack against her head. Then another. More came at her, like bugs swarming.

She looked up. Swirling throughout Olivia's modest living room were several dozen imps, each taking swipes at Samantha until she began to back off. She swatted at them, trying to search in her bag for a potion to stop them, but the imps were relentless. They pulled her hair, tried to pry off the bag from her shoulder, and one even made it into the bag, where it fished around through the potions.

Samantha swatted them off and considered if she could use her power on them again. It had been a long day and she was exhausted. Plus, there were more imps here than there had been earlier.

Out of the corner of her eye, Samantha saw something metallic come charging through the chaos from the kitchen. Before she had time to register what it was or act on it, the knife plunged into Olivia's chest.

"No!" Samantha cried out, jumping to assist Olivia. The knife likely went right through her lung, judging by the sudden gasping for air that Olivia was doing. If she pulled it out, Olivia would bleed to death. As it was, the alternative wasn't any better.

Behind the witches, the imps giggled maniacally, disappearing in a puff of smoke one-by-one.

"Olivia, look at me." Samantha kneeled beside her and tried to support her lolling head. "Focus on me. Keep your eyes open. We can get you help." She turned to her bag and rifled through her potions. "Maybe I have something that can heal—or something that can reverse…"

Her voice trailed off. She knew there was nothing in her bag that could save Olivia. Nothing she was equipped with that could change the way she failed her. How she didn't save her.

"We can get you to—" Samantha stopped short. Olivia's head drooped down, her chest soaked with blood that dripped onto the singed carpet.

Olivia was dead.

CHAPTER 14

It was as if Samantha were suspended from her body. She didn't remember letting out a roaring cry. She didn't know exactly when the tears started. And she only vaguely remembered Steven rushing in at the sound of the commotion and consoling her.

Steven wrapped his arms around her on the floor, shushing her, telling her everything was okay. That she was safe, that she did her best to save Olivia.

But had she?

Had she done everything in her power to save Olivia? Was this fate? Unable to be avoided? Shouldn't Samantha have sucked it up and asked for help? Either Kathy or Danielle or *someone*? Why did she think she'd be able to handle a force so powerful on her own—one she still didn't fully understand the greatness of?

"I could've done more." She sniffled.

"You did more than enough," he said. "This wasn't a direct threat on you or anyone in your family and you still stepped up and gave it your all anyway."

"But she died."

He sighed. "I know. But you could've too."

That reality suddenly came back to smack her in the face. It was true. She could've died. Possibly even Steven if he rushed up here at the wrong time. If those imps hadn't disappeared after killing Olivia, they could've turned on Samantha. Imps were something she could probably handle on her own, but there were so many of them. And it was the middle of the night and she was exhausted. And if she was gone, what was stopping them from turning on Steven? Or someone else in the building? Everything could've turned out very differently.

"I know," she whispered. "You were right. I was being reckless. I should've asked Kathy for help."

"You were brave," he corrected. "Sure, you got a little carried away. Thought you were invincible, but you're still here."

Samantha's eyes flickered to Olivia. "I wish I could say the same for her."

He squeezed her tighter. "You made a mistake. One that had serious consequences, sure, but you had the best intentions. In a way, you did save her. She never joined the Pentad. Never got taken advantage of. Never had to look over her shoulder for any threats to her life. The best you can do now it take what you've learned from this so next time you don't get in over your head."

She nodded. "From here on out, Kathy's going to be in on every magical outing."

Steven smoothed her hair out of her face and kissed the top of her head. "That's a good plan."

As she leaned in to him and let him comfort her, she couldn't help but think about everything she could've lost. It wasn't just her anymore. She had a husband now. A job. And, of course, the one constant in her life: Kathy. She needed to be more careful from now on.

Which meant that she had to tell Danielle that she needed to take a break from helping her with the Pentad. No more secret projects. Samantha had a life to preserve and, maybe someday, a family to protect.

CHAPTER 15

- MARCH 1, 1989 -
WEDNESDAY

It had been a whirlwind couple of weeks since Olivia had passed. Almost immediately after, Samantha and Kathy had been swept up in another magical issue, which left Samantha barely any time to recover from the first.

Besides that, there was another reason Samantha had been preoccupied. Something that made her nervous to share with Danielle. Which was why she hadn't talked to her friend from Salem as often as she used to. Their nightly phone calls had trickled to about once a week, with Samantha trying to build up the courage to tell the story of what happened with Olivia every time, but being too timid every phone call.

Over the last week alone, Danielle had called numerous times each night. Samantha was either busy, not home, or too tired to take the call. Now, however, after she had flipped over the calendar to March that morning and realized just how long it had been since Olivia's death, Samantha told herself to bite the bullet and pick up the phone.

"It's about time!" Danielle said on the other end when Samantha took the call. "Why haven't you been answering the phone? I've got a lot to tell you!"

"Hi, Danielle. How are you?" Samantha sat the kitchen table, the cord stretched across the room. She could tell her tone was heavy, weighed down by everything that had changed in the last couple weeks.

"I'm fine," Danielle said. "How are you doing?"

"Great—"

"Great! I've got a new lead, but you're going to have to take this one because it's—"

"I'm not sure how much longer I can do this," Samantha blurted. Do it quick, like a Band-Aid.

"What do you mean?"

Samantha leaned forward on the table, her hand rubbing her forehead to try to soothe the words she was about to say; the hurt she knew she would inflict on Danielle.

"You're the one who started this," Danielle said. "We're just scratching the surface of this group!"

Words like that didn't help Samantha feel any better.

"You're not preoccupied with some other evil thing, are you?" Danielle asked.

Samantha exhaled through her nose in a short chuckle. "No. This has nothing to do with that."

"Then what's the problem? I really need your help with this. The spirit branch is in Lily Dale, and I was thinking you—"

"I'm pregnant."

Silence.

After a minute, Samantha asked, "Are you still there?"

"I thought you wanted to wait to have kids?"

"It's not like we were trying, exactly. It just sort of came up." It had been a surprise to her. Something she was still wrapping her head around. "And I mean, besides all of this with the Pentad, I haven't been attacked too much. Very minor, low-level stuff. It's kind of perfect timing."

Another long pause, then, "So where does that leave us?"

Samantha sighed. She knew this conversation would be difficult. "Honestly, I think we should leave it alone for now. I've written a spell to kill Toxanna and put it in our magic book, just in case. I just think we should stop poking around and looking for trouble. We both know we're never short on that."

Danielle was quiet for a while. Both women let the changing dynamic of their friendship—and their lives—sink in.

"You're probably right." Danielle feigned breeziness, which only made Samantha feel guiltier. "Trouble will find us. Right now you need to take care of yourself. Your marriage. Your family. Use this time to freshen up on your abilities so that when evil comes back around, you'll be ready. I'm very happy for you. Congratulations."

"Thanks. Steven and I are really excited. My sister is over the moon to become an aunt."

"I bet," Danielle said with a hint of emotion in her voice. "Hey, look, I'm going to let you go. I'm sorry for bothering you these last few weeks. Once the baby comes, send me pictures."

"Of course. I'm really sorry about this. You've worked so hard and I feel like I'm ditching you, but…I've gotta take care of my family first, you know?"

"I know," Danielle said, clearly stuffed up all of a sudden.

When they ended the call, Samantha remained in the chair, with her fist pressed against her lips and the phone still clutched in her hand. She wished she could continue to help Danielle, but starting a family required sacrifices. Becoming a mother meant that Samantha couldn't take on everything like she used to try to. She needed to prioritize.

And if she had learned anything, it was that she needed to allow people to help her because she *couldn't* do it all. Olivia helped teach her that.

FROM THE AUTHOR OF THE UNDER THE MOON SERIES
DAVID NETH
Mayhem. It's what's for dinner.
HEX
COVEN: BOOK 9.5

CHAPTER 1

- NOVEMBER 1989 -

The temperature in the kitchen had to be a good ten degrees warmer than the rest of the house. Samantha had had the oven on since she got up at seven o'clock that morning and she'd been working up a storm ever since.

Samantha laid out the dough in a criss-cross pattern on the top of the cherry pie she had prepared. So far it looked good. The whole thing was from scratch—even the cherry filling. It was her first attempt at a true homemade pie, but she figured it was worth a try.

She found the recipe in one of those food magazines at the checkout line in the grocery store when she was buying the supplies for this feast. Hopefully it turned out good. It was the only dessert they had. Now that she was making it, though, she wondered if she should've made chocolate chip cookies or some other small dessert that was easier to munch on.

Samantha glanced up at the clock and saw that it was just after three o'clock. Their guests would be here in just two short hours and she still had to clean up the kitchen and shower and get herself ready for the meal.

"You're still cooking?" Kathy asked as she walked into the kitchen. She went straight for the fridge, which was filled to capacity with the breaded chicken, stuffing, green beans, salad, and various dressings. Not to mention the three bottles of wine, full pitcher of iced tea, and several bottles of water. "Whoa! Do we need to buy a second fridge?"

"Just get what you need and close the door," Samantha snapped. She finished laying out the dough on the top of the pie and breathed a sigh of relief. The last of the meal prep was done. Now she just needed to put it all in the oven at the appropriate times while also getting herself ready.

"Have you taken a seat at all today?" Kathy asked, opening a container of yogurt. Her hair was pulled up in a messy bun and she wore sweatpants and a plaid flannel shirt. "You're eight months pregnant, you should be taking it easy."

"I'm fully aware of the acrobat growing in my belly, thanks to all the bladder shots they've taken today." Samantha fussed with cleaning up the counter. She had wax paper, flour, and dirty dishes stacked everywhere.

"Is this dinner really worth it?" Kathy leaned against the

fridge and ate her yogurt. "Seems like a lot of work just to ask your boss for a raise."

"Yes, I know," Samantha admitted. She carried a stack of dishes to the sink and turned on the faucet to fill the pots with hot water. There were more than usual since she had to borrow from their extended stock of dishes to have enough for everything she was preparing. She poured a liberal amount of dish soap over all of them, hoping to cut down on the washing time.

"I just want to butter up Mr. Marsden before I ask him for a raise and then take a few months off for maternity leave," she said over her shoulder. "I don't want him to think that I'm taking advantage of him or the company."

"Based on what you've told me about what you do at work, I think you're more than earning your keep there," Kathy said. "Besides, you deserve to be paid a fair wage *and* be allowed time off for your family."

Samantha was nodding before her sister even finished. Meanwhile, she scooped up the extra flour that had piled on the counter and brushed it into the trash can. "I agree with you on all of that, but it just seems like a big ask with the situation." On her way back to the counter, she flicked the faucet off.

"You're nervous." Kathy licked her spoon clean and then tossed it with the dirty dishes. Her sister shot her a look. "What's another dish in this pile?"

"Easy for you to say," Samantha grumbled. Turning back to

the mess on the island, she continued, "Yes, I am nervous. And I want this dinner to be perfect. They've never been here before—and his wife hasn't ever met me. I want to leave a good first impression."

"Why did you invite them here to ask for a raise anyway? Wouldn't it have been easier to do it at the office after you've just impressed him with some long, boring report or something?" Kathy grinned at the jab.

Samantha made a guilty face and stepped to the sink to start on the dishes. "I want to appeal to his sympathy."

Kathy shook her head. "I'm not following." Then, she added with a nod to the sink, "Leave those. I'll do them for you."

"Are you sure?"

"Yeah. You need to take a break. All this working on your feet isn't good for my niece or nephew you're growing for me."

Samantha laughed as she absently rubbed her belly. "Oh yeah. I'm doing this *just* for you."

"Oh, you shouldn't have!" Kathy teased. "Now explain what you mean by appealing to your boss's sympathy. I'm not following."

"If he shows up and sees my house and my husband and we're talking about the baby and how excited we are for them to come, then he'll look at me as a woman who is trying to support her family and not an employee asking for more money."

The younger sister smiled with approval. "Oh,

manipulation! I like it!" She stepped to the sink and picked up a sponge. "You go get ready to impress. I've got these."

"You still need to change too. You look like you've been packing all day."

"I *have* been packing all day."

Kathy had just recently signed a lease on an apartment closer to downtown. It was the first time the two sisters wouldn't be living together, but it was time. Kathy was twenty-one now and had a steady job. Samantha was married with a baby on the way. They were adults. And that meant living apart.

"You didn't make a mess upstairs, did you?" Samantha asked. She didn't like to think about her little sister moving out, so she tended to deflect whenever the topic came up.

"No, everything's all tidy up there. The mess is in my bedroom, which I will close the door once I get up there to hide the mess."

"And you're going to have enough time to get yourself ready?"

"You said you wanted Mr. Marsden to see our home. I'm dressed very home*ly*!"

"Yes, but I don't want him to think my sister is home*less*."

Kathy's jaw dropped just before she burst into a laugh. "Mean!"

Samantha finished wiping up the counter with a sponge and then brought it back to the sink. "You sure you're okay doing these? There's a lot. I can get Steven to help. I had him outside making sure all the leaves were cleared from the yard, but I think he's done."

"Yes, Sam, I've got this under control. But hey, why are the potion pots and pans in here too?" There were pots that they exclusively used for potions because of the nature of many of the potion recipes. They didn't normally use those pots to cook with.

Samantha let out a heavy sigh. "Well…I tried to do a fancy cornbread bake thing, but that burnt in the oven. Then I wanted to do a green bean casserole, but I must've messed something up because that didn't turn out. I had used so many dishes that I had no choice but to pull those out. Don't worry, I scrubbed them real good to get the gunk off before I used them."

"Okay, well, I'll get the kitchen cleaned up for you," Kathy said. "You go up and take a shower and relax a little before they come."

Samantha pulled off her apron and strung it on the hook on the back of the basement door. "I'm not sure I'll be able to relax, but I'll take you up on your offer to clean." She gave her sister a quick squeeze from behind, which was hindered by her large belly, and then disappeared up the stairs.

CHAPTER 2

T his stupid cork!" Samantha groaned as she struggled with the corkscrew at the top of the wine bottle.

"Do you want me to get it?" Steven offered from the other end of the dining room table. He was arranging silverware on top of folded napkins. The salad already sat in the bowl on the table, next to two candle sticks—yellow, which was supposed to encourage persuasion. And confidence. Two things that she hoped were in abundant amounts over the course of the evening.

"No, I've got it," his wife grumbled as she continued to struggle.

"Sam, I can do it—"

The doorbell rang. The couple looked at each other, then at the door.

HEX

"Was that the door already?" Kathy asked, coming out of kitchen while drying her hands in a dish towel. It was an odd sight, with her dressed in a nice dress and heels.

"They're early," Steven said. He was dressed in a blue blazer and khakis—an outfit that Samantha had picked out for him the night before. "We're supposed to have another fifteen minutes."

"Well, it's not like I'm going to leave them standing on the front steps." Samantha handed her sister the bottle of wine with the corkscrew still sticking out of the top. "Here. Open this, but don't pour any glasses until they say they want it. We're not forcing them to drink if they're not comfortable."

"I'm on it." Kathy disappeared back into the kitchen.

Steven caught his wife by the arm as she marched to the door. "Hey, take a deep breath and try to relax before we let them in."

Samantha nodded and took a quick breath. "Okay. Ready? We should answer the door together."

"Sam, I'm serious."

"I know. And I know you mean well, but *telling* me to relax is—surprisingly—not going to help me relax." She hooked her elbow around his. "Just, please, try to make this night go as smoothly as I've planned it. Okay?"

Knowing how stressed out she was about the evening, Steven conceded to his wife's demands and nodded.

Mr. Marsden and his wife smiled when the Harpers greeted them at the door.

"Hi!" Samantha said with a big smile. "Come on in."

"Here, let me take your coats," Steven offered as their guests stepped inside.

Mr. Marsden and his wife each handed Steven their outerwear and then looked around the house. "Samantha, this is beautiful!"

"So well-preserved!" his wife commented.

"Thank you," Samantha said with a smile. "It's a family home. We've had it for generations."

"Oh my, imagine all of the stories if these walls could talk!" Mr. Marsden's wife said.

Samantha didn't have to imagine. She knew quite a bit about what had gone on in this house and all of the magical adventures and mishaps.

"Samantha, this is my wife, Lucille," Mr. Marsden introduced.

"And this is my husband, Steven," she said. "My sister, Kathy, is in the kitchen. She'll be out in a minute."

Lucille stepped further into the living room. Samantha had been through the whole house the day before, immaculately cleaning every nook and cranny. The living room was spotless, with the large comfortable furniture situated around an ornate brick fireplace with ceramic tiles on the hearth. It was flanked by two wooden bookshelves that her grandfather had made in his workshop out in the garage.

"So just how old is this house?" Lucille asked.

"It was built in the 1870s, so nearly one hundred and twenty years now," Samantha said. "Would you two like a tour while we wait for dinner?"

Lucille brightened at the idea. "Oh, I would love that!"

"If you don't mind," Mr. Marsden replied.

"Steven, honey, why don't you get these two each a glass of wine." Samantha quickly turned back to her boss and his wife. "If you would like, that is."

"If it's no trouble," Mr. Marsden said.

"Not at all," she replied. Then, telepathically, she pushed into her husband's mind: *Get the drinks pouring so the alcohol can help soften the blow of what I'm about to ask him.*

Steven shot his wife a look just before he turned to head into the kitchen. He hated when she used her telepathic abilities on him, but it's not like she was reading his thoughts. Only projecting her own into his.

"So this is the living room, obviously," Samantha said, starting the tour for the Marsdens. "It's one of our favorite rooms in the house since it's one of the few that's actually a lounging area."

"Really? You don't have a library or a den or anything?" Lucille asked. "I volunteer at the Historical Society and a lot of regal older homes like these have several gathering areas. It was a social class thing back in the day. Thankfully, we've mostly outgrown that idea as a society."

Samantha smiled. "How interesting. No, in this house we

have just the basics, really." She indicated the door that was closed off. "The sunroom through that door and the dining room are about as fancy as we get. The sunroom is pretty much shut up for the winter. Too drafty with the original windows and replacing all of them would cost a fortune."

Less talk about money, she scolded herself.

"Oh, I'd imagine," Mr. Marsden said. "We just did our windows last summer and it hurt to write that check."

"You said this house was built in the 1870s?" Lucille asked. Samantha nodded.

"Did the city limits even reach that far back then?"

"Funny enough, no. Actually, currently we're pretty much at the edge of the city proper. Back when this was built, though, this wasn't even in the city. Here's a little history lesson for you—Lucille, you probably already know this—the city was officially incorporated in 1851, so when this house was built twenty years later, it was really just a farmhouse. It had been added on to a few times, especially once they laid out the street grid in this area—so the house looked like it always fit. It's grandeur was added piece-by-piece over time as my family gained wealth."

More talk of money, Samantha noted.

"And how long did that take?" Mr. Marsden asked. "To add on, that is?"

"Well, it was my great-great-grandparents who first built the house, and by the time my grandparents had possession of it, it looked pretty much like this," Samantha explained. "I only know what my father told me, and he only knew what he remembered growing up here and what *his* parents told him."

The memory of her father was sad, especially with her pregnant belly serving as a constant reminder of what he was missing out on, but she changed tacts to keep her mind off of it.

Samantha continued the tour, naming off where different things in the house had been sourced from originally. Paintings, tiles, woodwork, everything that she could think of, she mentioned. She even took them upstairs to show them the bedrooms and how much detail each of those had, despite them not being common rooms. The one room she stayed out of was Kathy's bedroom, where her mess lay hidden behind the solid-core door.

The last stop on the tour was the nursery, which they had just finished putting together the previous weekend. That started talk about the baby and when Samantha was due and all of the hubbub surrounding that.

By the time Samantha had led them back down to the dining room, Steven was waiting with glasses of wine and Kathy was in the midst of bringing the food to the table.

"Oh, and this is my sister, Kathy," Samantha said. "Kathy, these are the Marsdens."

Kathy came around the table to shake their hands. "Nice to meet you both. Oh, I love your necklace," she added to Lucille.

"Thank you! My sister bought it for me."

"We've heard so much about you already tonight," Mr. Marsden said.

"Uh oh," Kathy said with a grin.

"You two are very close," Lucille said. "I admire that."

"Thank you," Samantha said for them both.

The room fell into an awkward quiet, for only a second. Noticing it, Kathy sprung into action.

"Please, everybody, sit!" she turned to the table and gestured at the chairs. "Everything's ready. The wine is poured. Take any seat you'd like!"

Samantha mouthed a thank you to her sister as they moved around the table.

"Oh shoot," Samantha said. "We don't have serving spoons. Kathy, can you help me bring some out?"

Kathy eyed her sister, but smiled politely at their guests and followed her sister to the kitchen.

CHAPTER 3

That wasn't very subtle," Kathy said when she and Samantha were alone in the kitchen.

"I'm freaking out!" Samantha said in a whisper-shout. "What's the matter?"

"I just rambled on and on about the house, as if I was some kind of tour-guide!"

Kathy rolled her eyes. "You're being dramatic. I think everything's going great. The Marsdens really seemed interested in what you had to say about the house." She stepped to the oven and checked on the pie that was warming. The wonderful cherry aromas were now adding the scents filling the kitchen.

"It was all so self-centered," Samantha went on. "Me, me,

me, me, me. I didn't ask them anything about them! Lucille even volunteers at the Historical Society! It was the perfect segue into learning about them."

"Sam, relax. They don't seem the least bit annoyed with you." She smirked. "Me, on the other hand…"

Samantha ran both hands under her hair and rubbed the back of her neck. "Seriously, that's not helping."

"And obsessing over every detail of this evening isn't helping either," Kathy said. "Not for what you want to ask Mr. Marsden and certainly not for the baby. Besides, are you going to keep dragging me in here to freak out about every little thing when what you should be doing is sitting out there with them and schmoozing your boss every moment you can?"

Taking a deep breath, Samantha nodded. "You're right. I need to calm down and I focus on what this evening is all about."

"That's better."

"So you think it's going well, though?"

"Hey, I've only just met them. But yeah, I think it's going great." Kathy rocked her head back and forth. "I mean, taking them up to see the bedrooms was a little strange, but you pulled it off nicely by talking about the baby."

Samantha groaned and sunk into a chair. "I know! Do you think it's obvious that I want to ask him for something? That I'm just buttering him up? Maybe this whole thing was a mistake."

Hex

Kathy grabbed her sister's arms and squeezed. "Take three deep breaths." She paused, waiting for Samantha to comply. Finally, she did and Kathy continued. "Better?"

Samantha shrugged.

"Look, everything's fine. Admittedly, you did go a little overboard with everything—the meal, dictating what Steven and I wear, cleaning the house, *touring* the house—"

"Okay, I get it."

"Sorry. But even with all of that, I don't think there's any harm in having your boss and his wife over for a nice dinner. And even if he does suspect you want to ask him something, so what? Maybe he'll enjoy the company just the same. Relax and make the most of the evening that you put together."

Samantha nodded, then turned to look out the doorway into the dining room. "I hope it's not dead silence out there. Do you think they can hear us?"

"Of course not," Kathy said. "Besides, Steven knows how important this night is to you and how much you've worked to make this dinner a success. He's probably doing his best to schmooze the two of them as we speak. He'd do a better job of it with you there, though."

"You're right. And thank you for finishing dinner. I really appreciate it."

"Hey, we've got your back."

Samantha smiled and took another deep breath. "Thank you."

David Neth

"Of course." Kathy leaned over and hugged her older sister. "Now go back out there and let's impress the pants off of them until Mr. Marsden agrees to give you that raise."

CHAPTER 4

To Samantha's relief, conversation during dinner was pretty easy. It was mostly simple small talk, but none of it felt forced or awkward. Kathy talked about what she did for work, Steven described some of the clients he had on his caseload at his office, and Samantha discussed their plans for when the baby came.

"Now how long have you two been married now?" Lucille asked.

Samantha and Steven looked at each other before she answered, "Ten months, I guess. Seems like it's been a lot longer than that. So much has happened since then." She looked down at her belly. "I can't imagine why."

Everyone laughed.

"You two didn't waste any time!" Mr. Marsden joked.

His wife swatted at him. "Honey! Don't be rude." She turned back to the hosts. "If you don't mind me asking, when did the two of you start dating?"

"Let's see," Steven said, "we first got together during my second year of college, so that would've been…1985?" He looked to his wife for confirmation and she nodded. "So almost five years now."

"And we were engaged for about six months before we got married," Samantha added.

"How did he propose?" Lucille leaned on her clasped hands under her chin with a sly grin on her face.

"It was actually right after I got this job," Samantha said. She wondered if this was a good time to bring up the raise, but then, that would be dodging Lucille's question and that just seemed rude. "He took me out to dinner and that's when he asked me."

"Nothing too crazy," Steven added.

"Oh, but that's so sweet!" Lucille said.

"I joke that Steven wanted a small audience to make it harder for Samantha to turn him down," Kathy said with a smirk.

"Oh please," Steven said. "It was always a yes, wasn't it, Sam?" He pulled her closer to him and kissed the top of her head.

She looked up and said, "Well…" A smile broke out on her face. "Of course, dear. I knew we were going to be together forever long before we ever made it official."

"Ugh, this is why I need my own place," Kathy murmured. "All this PDA has me feeling like a third wheel."

Samantha tossed her sister a warning look and Kathy bit her top lip to hold in any further comments.

Mr. Marsden put his arm behind Lucille's chair and smiled at his wife. "Why don't you tell them our story, honey? About how I proposed?"

She started laughing before she even began. "My husband, here, tried to be romantic. He invited me over to his apartment for dinner, where he made this elaborate feast. Obviously, right away I knew that *something* was up. Barely knows his way around the kitchen and suddenly here he was making a full meal for the two of us?"

Samantha felt herself grow hot, even as she tried to maintain her calm demeanor. The fancy meal, the unexpected dinner invitation, the flattery and small talk. Were they on to her plan?

"Hey, I spent a lot on that meal," he cut in. "Time and money. I'd never really cooked before."

"Like I said, I knew something was up." Everyone laughed. "But everything was delicious. He did a wonderful job." Lucille patted her husband's hand.

"…until I brought out the red wine."

They both chuckled again.

"He handed me my glass and I took a sip—only to find that

he had put the ring in the wine," Lucille said.

"She shrieked so loud—"

"Spilled the wine all over the table—"

"Thought there was a bug in the glass—"

"When I finally calmed down, he showed me the ring," she said.

"At that point, the tablecloth was stained and there was food all over the floor."

She looked lovingly at her husband. "But it was an easy yes once he finally asked."

"And the rest, as they say, is history." Mr. Marsden took his wife's hand and kissed the back of it.

"Aw, that's so cute!" Kathy said. "I hope that someday I have a story like that to tell. I'm currently striking out in the romance department."

"It'll come to you when it's meant to," Lucille said. "Don't you worry."

Steven snickered. Samantha kicked him under the table, knowing what he was thinking about Kathy's tumultuous love life.

"Actually, I had a pretty serious relationship for a while, but we broke up in the spring," Kathy said. "It's for the best, really, but—"

Mr. Marsden let out a loud belch and everyone stared at the sudden noise. He brought a fist to his mouth, then patted his chest.

"Sorry. I'm not really sure where that came from."

"Would you like a glass of water?" Samantha asked.

"No, I think I'll be—" Another loud belch escaped him.

Lucille rubbed his shoulders. "Are you okay, dear?"

"The bathroom's just around the corner," Steven said.

Mr. Marsden nodded, still tapping his fist on his chest to stifle any other bodily functions. He hiccuped, and then burped loudly again.

Don't tell me I gave everyone food poisoning, Samantha worried. *What a way to ask for a raise!* Her heart was hammering in her chest at a mile a minute.

"I'll get you that water." Kathy rose from her seat and disappeared into the kitchen.

Mr. Marsden continued to hiccup and burp. His wife began slapping his back, trying to help.

"I'm so sorry about—"

"Don't be," Samantha said. "It's not like you can help it. Maybe some fresh air would help? Or maybe—"

"Here you go!" Kathy trilled as she returned with a full glass of water.

Mr. Marsden burped again before he could take the glass. He pushed away from the table.

"Honey, are you sure you're all right?"

He shook his head. "I'm feeling…funny."

"Funny?" Lucille asked. "Funny how?"

Great, Samantha thought. *He's going to vomit all over the table!*

What happened next was much worse than her boss getting sick. Instead, with the next belch, his entire body floated right out of his chair and up toward the ceiling like a helium balloon.

CHAPTER 5

"Honey!" Lucille shrieked as she stood up from her seat, her eyes glued to her husband floating up near the ceiling. "How did you get up there?"

"I don't know!"

Samantha and Kathy exchanged looks, silently asking the same question.

The older witch turned to her own husband. "Steven, can you keep them—Steven?"

Her husband slumped to the floor, narrowly missing the edge of the table as he collapsed.

"Steven!" Samantha cried out. "Are you okay?" She knelt down next to him, tucking her hair behind her ears as she did so. Soon, a puzzled look came over her.

"What is it?" Kathy asked, while the Marsdens continued to shout at each other from across the table.

"He's asleep," Samantha told her.

"Was he tired?"

"Not that I know of. And he only had about half a glass of wine."

"I'm going to go out on a limb and say that this isn't because he's a lightweight."

Samantha glared at her sister and then turned back to Steven. Closer inspection revealed that he didn't seem to hurt himself in his fall. As she leaned over his head to make sure he wasn't bleeding, she jumped when he began snoring loudly.

Kathy laughed, but sucked in her lips when Samantha shot her a look. "Sorry. It just seemed fun."

"What on *earth* is going on here?" Lucille demanded of the sisters.

They turned to her, at a loss for words.

"Lucille—Mrs. Marsden—you see, this isn't—this is just…" Samantha trailed off. She had no explanation for the woman, real or fabricated.

In desperation, she turned to Kathy to help fill in for what she couldn't. Soon, Samantha's eyes grew wide again as she watched her sister's lips elongate, flatten, and turn a yellowish-orange color. A duck beak.

"What?" Kathy asked with a nasally tone.

Lucille let out another shriek, and then she herself fell to the floor.

"What is it?" Kathy insisted, the pitch of her voice increasing as panic overwhelmed her.

"Your…your…" All Samantha could do was motion to her own mouth.

"Huh?" With shaking hands, Kathy reached up and felt for her lips. When her fingers grazed her new beak, she let out a quick shout. "Ah!" She sucked in a deep breath. "Okay! Okay. So we need to shigure out—shigure out—*shigure*." She shook her head, frustrated that she was unable to pronounce the "f" sound with her new beak. "We need to shix this! *Now!*"

Samantha nodded, stifling her own grin.

"It's not shunny!" Kathy whined.

The absurdity of the whole evening finally got to Samantha and she lost herself in her laughter.

"Sanantha!" Kathy tried to sound stern, but mispronouncing her "m" only added to her sister's laugh. "Shine! You shigure this out on your own!"

Samantha reached for Kathy and pulled her back, her giggles subsiding. "No, I'm sorry. I shouldn't have laughed."

Kathy crossed her arms and looked at her.

"I'm sorry!" Samantha pleaded. "You're right. We need to figure out what happened. Because something *did* happened to everyone."

"Exceth you and Lucille."

"So far. Book?"

"Owiously." Kathy started to the stairs in a march, only stopping when Samantha let out a shout from behind her. "What?"

"Something's…blocking me or something," Samantha said from just inside the dining room. She took a step forward, but ran into an invisible wall.

Kathy waved her hand in the space between the foyer and the dining room, then looked at her sister with skepticism. "There's nothing there."

"Why would I lie about not being able to make it through the doorway? I'm telling you, something's blocking me!"

Again, Kathy stepped between the two rooms with no issues. "Are you sure?"

"Yes! Here, let me try something." Stepping over the legs of her husband, Samantha got a running start of a few feet. She charged toward the cased opening, slamming hard against something invisible that seemed to run right down the line where Kathy was standing. The force knocked her back on the floor beside Steven.

"Oh," Kathy said plainly. "Looks like you're stuck."

"*Just* me." Samantha shot her sister a look as she picked herself up off the floor. She rubbed her belly absently, happy to feel the baby kick. That was the last thing she needed. An invisible magical force field hurting her baby in the womb.

"So now what?"

"We have to figure it out. *Some* kind of magic is happening here."

"Wut it's weird that it's not the same thing shor all osh us," Kathy said. "Ewaryone is eshected disherently."

"So you're going to have to get the book and bring it down to me so we can figure out what's going on," Samantha said. "Soon, before Lucille wakes up."

Kathy nodded and raced up the stairs.

Samantha watched her sister disappear up the stairs. She already felt claustrophobic from not being able to leave the room. Simply the knowledge of it seemed to make her feel stuck.

"Uh…" a voice said from the other room.

Samantha's head snapped around and saw it was Mr. Marsden up on the ceiling. She had forgotten about him.

"What the hell is going on!?"

CHAPTER 6

U m…" Samantha's mouth hung open as she looked up at her boss on the ceiling. "That's a great question!"

"What did you do to me?" Mr. Marsden demanded. "How did I just float up to the ceiling? What did you put in our dinner?"

That's an even better question, Samantha thought to herself.

To her relief, she didn't have to respond to her boss's request for answers. Kathy came down the stairs, which drew his attention.

"You! Maybe you'll answer me!" Mr. Marsden said to Kathy. "What is—"

Before he even finished his question, Kathy raised her hand and froze him in mid-air.

HEX

Samantha shrugged at the ease of use of Kathy's magic. At least their powers were still intact.

"Naywe now we can shinally *think* without any interruhtions," she murmured.

"Thanks for that," Samantha said. "I have no idea how we're going to explain any of this away."

"Shirst, let's try to shigure out *why* all of this is hahhening, then how to rewerse it." Kathy pushed aside the dirty plates on the dining room table and set the magic book down. "Ashter that, we can worry awout exhlaining it."

Samantha ran her hands over the silvery lettering on the cover that read: *The Art of Magic*. It was every bit of knowledge their family had gathered on all things magical over generations. Even with all of that, Samantha had her doubts that there would be an answer in the book for how to solve their problems.

"Okay, so I think the shirst hlace to check is us," Kathy said. She motioned to her new beak. "I nean, clearly I'we wen ashected wy whatewer's going on, but naywe ny howers are sonehow the cause osh it too."

Samantha raised an eyebrow. "We need to fix that beak, because it's getting harder to understand you." She took a deep breath. "Anyway, I think I got the gist of what you meant. The problem is, I don't see it. You have a time specialty, not a transmogrification specialty. Besides, how does that answer my boss hanging out on the ceiling or

Steven passing out for no reason?"

Kathy shrugged. "I don't know. I was just shitwalling."

"Shitwalling?" Samantha asked.

"You know what I neant! Wrainstorning! Throwing out randon ideas!"

The older witch shook her head at her sister's fractured speech. "Whatever. The other thing is, look at Mr. Marsden! You froze him without any issues. Your powers are obviously fine."

"Then what awout yours? You can't leawe this roon, wut otherwise you're shine. Naywe it's your powers that's doing all of this. You *hawe* wen stressed out awout this dinner shor a while." *Maybe it's your powers mixing with the baby's powers*, Kathy thought in her own head, which Samantha read with his mind specialty.

"Not every magical issue is related to the baby in my belly! Something else is going on here. We just need to figure out what that is."

Kathy flipped the book absently. "It's just weird that this is hahhening. It's not like we're under attack."

"Or are we?" Samantha crossed her arms and rolled her eyes. "What a night to strike. Maybe whatever enemy we're facing has been watching us. Maybe they knew we'd be distracted tonight and figured that was the best time to get us."

"Aren't we always distracted, though?" Kathy asked. "Wut we always shigure it out and we always win."

"There's a first time for everything, though," Samantha said.

Hex

Kathy continued to flip through pages in the book. "Don't we so hessinistic. I nean, really, the attack angle doesn't really nake sense. Why would soneone choose these nishaps over other ohtions? I nean, what disherence does it nake ish I hawe a weak when I'n osh awle nind and ny howers work just shine? And why send Nr. Narsden uh to the ceiling when Stewen just went into a deeh sleeh and Lucille wasn't eshected at all?"

Samantha could see her sister's point. "Okay, so what does that leave us with?"

"Naywe this was just an unshortunate accident."

"An *accident*?" Samantha blurted. "How can this be an—" She stopped herself as Mr. Marsden's own words replayed in her mind. *What did you put in our dinner?* "That's it."

"What?" Kathy asked. "I'n not the one who's the nind reader here."

"The food."

"It was hoisoned?"

Samantha shot her sister a quick look. "Of course it wasn't poisoned. I made it! No, I think it was tainted."

"Isn't that the sane thing as hoisoned? Just…not intentional?"

The older sister let out a heavy sigh. "What I'm saying is, maybe something got into the food without us realizing and the varying amounts had different effects on different people."

"Wut what kind of nagic would hawe that eshect?"

"Potions," Samantha said. "I used the potions pots for

dinner. And they're made out of cast iron—"

"Which neans it holds in flawor nore—or in this case, nagic," Kathy finished. "So it looks like you did hoison us ashter all."

CHAPTER 7

ind anything?" Samantha asked from the dining room.

In the kitchen, Kathy sat on the floor with the lower cabinet doors open, inspecting the potions pots that she had scrubbed and cleaned earlier while Samantha was getting ready for this disastrous dinner. The pots lay scattered on the floor around her.

"Nothing that I can shind," she said. She hiccuped and a flat squeak came out. Almost like a—

"Did you just quack?" Samantha asked.

Kathy put a hand on the end of her beak. "No…" At least, she hoped not. "The hots look shine, Sam. They're the sane ones we'we wen using for years and years."

"That's the problem. All those potion ingredients and

incantations spoken over those pots, it's a wonder even our potions turn out right." She let out a heavy sigh and slumped against the doorframe as Kathy returned to the dining room. "I can't believe I didn't even *think* of that. How stupid of me!"

"Wlaning yourselsh isn't going to helh anything," Kathy said. "It was an honest nistake. How could you hawe known that the hotions had worked their way into the hots thenselwes?"

"Because that's what cast iron does! It's why people use them to cook with, to take advantage of the flavoring from all the meals previously cooked in them."

She let out a heavy breath, hoping that it would help calm her—she'd been doing that a lot this evening. Unfortunately, even this attempt at relaxing had the same effect as the other. Useless.

"Those pots have been used by our family for potions forever," she went on. "They were probably created at a blacksmith shop back in the day. Probably when this was just a simple farmhouse. We're talking more than a hundred years of magic stored in them. No wonder we're having such wonky side effects."

"Okay, so we hawe some weird side eshects—"

"These aren't just some *weird* side effects!" Samantha blurted. "Kathy, you have a beak! You're talking like Donald Duck! What part of this is simply 'weird'?"

"You're right, wut they're really not that bad when you think about it."

Samantha rolled her eyes. "My boss is on the ceiling! My husband has turned into freaking sleeping beauty! And I've been imprisoned in my dining room for the rest of my life. Oh sure, Kathy, this is *not that bad*."

"They could we dead."

"That's a pretty low bar to set."

"Look, all I'n saying is that these side eshects—while inconwenient and annoying—are hretty nild. And we know what they are. The reality is—" She hiccuped again and let out a distinct quack.

Samantha couldn't help but smile. The quack and the beak only added to the madness of the whole evening.

Kathy took a deep breath to restart. "Ewerything is shixawle."

"How?"

"You're the hotions naster of the fanily, right?"

Samantha shrugged.

"So you're the west herson to answer the question: Do you think all of this nagic can be rewersed?"

The older witch thought about it. "That's a very good question."

CHAPTER 8

Kathy shook her head as she flipped through the pages of *The Art of Magic*. "No," she murmured, first to herself and then to her sister. "No. Nothing is hohhing out at ne as a way to shix this."

"As nice as it would be, we know we're not going to find a one-spell-fits-all approach," Samantha said. "Each issue is different."

"And it's not like you could whih uh a hotion that would allewiate any of these," Kathy said. "Wecause you can't cross a threshold."

"Exactly."

The sisters were both trying to have a positive attitude about the situation, but it was hard when they really only had one room to search for solutions. And that one room happened to be surrounded by everything that they needed to fix.

Kathy laid her hands out on the ancient pages and stared up at Mr. Marsden frozen near the ceiling. "Okay. I guess I could try to con uh with a shell to rewerse each unique use of nagic."

"We don't really have time for that—and we're not even sure it's going to work. I'd rather not use experimental spells, especially with people like my husband and my boss."

"So what do we do then?"

Samantha tucked her hair behind her ears and crossed her arms as she thought. After a minute, she said, "Turn to the section on potions."

"I thought we said we can't use a hotion wecause you can't nake one." Kathy searched for the correct section of the book as she spoke.

"No, but you can."

"Ne?" Kathy gave her sister an incredulous look, made worse by the duck beak she sported.

"I think there's a potion recipe in there for undoing transmogrifications."

"I'n not even going to attenht that word with ny weak." After flipping through a few more pages, she said, "Here it is. Are you sure I can do this? I hawen't worked with hotions a lot, and the ones that I hawe done hawe wen shlohs."

"Flops?" Samantha asked for clarification. She had mostly gotten he hang of Kathy's duck-speak, but there were some words that she couldn't figure out. Even in context.

Kathy nodded that the word was correct.

"Well, you'll just have to do better with this one."

"No hressure or anything."

"You can do it. Besides, if you screw up that one it's only your face."

Kathy shot her sister a look.

"Sorry. I just thought humor would put us both at ease. There should be a sleeping potion in there too."

"A sleehing hotion for what?"

"Because Steven's asleep."

"Wut don't you want to rewerse that?"

"Just find the potion and I'll see if my idea is even possible."

Turning a few more pages, Kathy found it.

Samantha sat next to her sister and pulled the book closer so she could read through the recipe. She scanned the list of ingredients and then tapped the page. "Lavender. That has to be it."

"Why?"

"Lavender is used for sleep potions, among other things."

"And you were just wrewing uh sleeh hotions lesht and right?" Kathy asked.

"No, but I did whip up something with lavender in it for love, protection, and peace. I've been mixing it in my tea at night. Figured it could only help with the baby."

"So how do we rewerse it? Otherwise, your huswand is

going to sleeh through the wirth of your child. Currently, he's serwing nore hurhose as a shloor nat."

Samantha smacked her sister's arm. "I'll come up with a recipe that can reverse it."

"So you're hawing ne nake *two* hotions now?"

"Relax. The reversal for the sleeping potion will probably just be mixing yew in his drink. The tricky part will be getting it into him."

"What does yew do?"

"It's used in necromancy."

"Raising the dead? He's out, San, wut he's not *dead*."

"It can also be used for resurrection and breaking hexes," Samantha explained. "It should work. Hopefully."

"Hoheshully?"

"Well, it's not like it's going to hurt him!"

Kathy let out a heavy sigh. "Okay. And what awout your walloon woss?"

Samantha looked up at Mr. Marsden, still frozen by Kathy's magic near the ceiling. Her power would likely be wearing off anytime now. "I can't think of any potion that would reverse that kind of magic. You're going to have to write a spell."

Kathy shook her head. "No. Ish I'n wusy naking two hotions, you're going to hawe to con uh with the shell to shix your woss."

"You know words don't come easy to me," Samantha

admitted quietly. Like anyone, she hated pointing out her shortcomings.

"They don't con easy to ne right now, either!" Kathy indicated her beak.

"True."

"Look, ish I hawe to get ower the whole hotions thing, you hawe to get ower the shell thing."

"Fair enough," Samantha agreed. "But what about me? How are we going to get me to pass through a doorway?"

Kathy tapped the end of her yellow beak. "Hold on, I'll we right wack."

"Where are you going?" Samantha called after her sister, who raced up the stairs.

No response came and Samantha looked around at the mess that had become her dinner party. What a motley crew they had turned out to be. And what a disaster. She didn't even want to begin to think about how they were going to explain all of this to the Marsdens. And when was Lucille going to wake up from her brief stint of unconsciousness?

Kathy came back down holding a golden metal medallion that had been patinated after years in storage. "Here. Try this."

"What is that?" Samantha reluctantly took it from her sister.

"Hut it on. It's a talisnan."

"That does what?" With ginger hands, Samantha clipped it behind her neck and felt the cold metal against her skin.

"I'n hretty sure it renowes any nagic that had wen hut on soneone," Kathy said.

"You're *pretty sure*?"

"It night take a little while for anything to take eshect, though. It's kind of old."

Talismans were magical instruments that were once regular objects that had been enchanted by a witch's magic. Unlike amulets, which were magic in and of themselves and got stronger with age, talismans sometimes lost their power the longer it went from the initial spell the witch had cast on it.

"Let's hope it doesn't do anything to the baby."

"Like what?" Kathy asked. "Either it works or it doesn't. You—and the wawy—will we shine. Now, ish we want eweryone else to we shine too, we need to get to work."

CHAPTER 9

Kathy blew her frizzy hair out of her face for the third time. The steam from the potions she had been brewing—coupled with the fact that she had had to run out to the dining room and freeze the Marsdens twice after her magic wore off—had melted away all of the time and effort she had put into her appearance.

Oh well, she thought to herself. *What difference does it really make if we can't reverse this and the Marsdens find out we're witches anyway?*

Relieved to be done creating the two different potions on her own, Kathy bottled each of them up and carried the vials out into the dining room to rejoin her sister. She would worry about cleaning up the dishes for the potion later, even though the foul stench wafted throughout the house. After all, she had already made a mess of the kitchen when she pulled out all the potions pots and pans to inspect them earlier. What was another mess to top off the evening?

"All set?" Samantha asked from the table. The older sister was hunched over a notepad, several wads of balled up paper scattered the floor around her.

"I think so. Hoheshully they actually work." Kathy set the vials on the table.

"Well, one of them is for you, so you're the one who has to worry the most."

"And the other is shor the shather of your child," Kathy replied. "So we're equally inwested. Actually, Stewen has a higher risk of hawing ewen nore side eshects since you whihhed uh that rewersal in a natter of ninutes."

Samantha waved her hand at that statement. "It's all just a matter of putting in the same basic components and adding a few extras to do what you want it to do."

"Oh, so sinhle." Kathy rolled her eyes. "I hated ewery ninute of wrewing that hotion."

"And you think I'm faring any better with these spells?"

"What do you hawe so shar?" Kathy peered over her sister's shoulder to read what she had on the notepad. "Hmm."

"Terrible, right? The grammar is all wrong."

"I nean, that's not really a wig issue. It's nagic, not rocket science. Wut I think you're doing too nuch."

"Too much?" Samantha asked. "I want to make sure that there's no wiggle room for errors! This is my boss!"

"Yes, I'n wery aware of who he is," Kathy muttered. "Look, just keeh the shirst two lines and I think that will do it."

"Are you sure?"

"Yeah. It states exactly what you want it to do. Wesides, half of the spell is the intention of the caster. That's why sonetines hershectly good shells still go wrong. Ish the caster doesn't know what they truly want it to do, then the hower wehind the shell is held wack, so to sheak."

"Interesting. Should we cast it together for some extra *oomph*?"

Kathy shrugged. "Couldn't hurt. I should hrowawly get rid of the weak shirst, so I can use ny real woice and not this quacking one." She reached for the vial and then paused.

"What's the matter?" Samantha asked. "Did you forget which one is which?"

"No, that's not it."

"Nervous?"

Kathy nodded. "Can we try the other one on Stewen shirst?"

Samantha shot her sister a look. "We're not playing guinea pig with my husband. Just drink it."

Sighing, Kathy popped open the cork and downed the vile concoction. She shook her head back and forth at the bad taste and felt a wave of nausea, but soon the feeling passed and she could feel her face return to normal. For good measure, she pawed at her restored lips with both hands and rushed to a mirror to double-check that everything was back the way it should be.

"Finally!"

"Relax, you only had the beak for, like, an hour." Samantha grabbed the second vial and kneeled on the floor beside her husband. Putting a hand behind his neck, she tilted his chin up so she could pour the potion in. The last time she did this maneuver to someone else, it was in Buffalo when she stripped another witch's powers. That was back when she only suspected she was pregnant. So much had changed in such a short time.

With the potion in his mouth, Steven first started coughing, then opened his eyes and sat up. He pounded at his chest with his fist as his body reacted to the potion. Samantha patted him on the back for good measure.

"You okay?" she asked. "You're not sleepy, are you?"

"Sleepy?" he asked between coughs. "No, I'm choking!"

"Here, take a sip of water." Kathy handed him his glass from the table.

After a few big gulps, Steven's cough subsided and then he looked between the two women. "So I'm guessing from the fact that I'm on the floor that your dinner didn't go exactly as you had planned?" He reached for the talisman hanging from Samantha's neck. "What's this?"

"It's something that's supposed to break whatever hex was accidentally put on me that keeps me from walking through doorways," Samantha said. "Oh, and Mr. Marden is stuck up on the ceiling and Kathy just got rid of her beak."

Steven's head snapped to the younger witch.

"It was weird," Kathy told him.

"So yeah," Samantha added. "Nothing about tonight went as planned. Now I just want to get them out of here without anymore suspicion of witchcraft."

Steven used the table to help himself get back on his feet, then offered his hand to Samantha to help her up. With her large belly, getting up from anywhere even was more difficult than usual.

"What are you doing?" Samantha asked her sister when she was back on her feet.

Kathy was over by Lucille, looking around on the floor. "Something's been bothering me about this whole thing. How come everyone had something happen to them as a result from the potion remnants, but not her?"

"Maybe she didn't get a high enough dosage," Samantha suggested.

"Mmm, I'm not sure." The younger witch knelt down beside Lucille, but something beneath the table caught her eye. "Aha!"

"What is it?" Samantha moved around the table to look for herself.

"She hasn't eaten a single thing! Look at this!" Kathy held up a folded napkin for Samantha to see.

HEX

Buried inside the napkin were parts of the chicken Samantha had served.

"And there's potatoes in the soil of this plant!" Kathy declared.

"Wow," Steven muttered.

"What a bitch!" Samantha looked to Lucille, outraged. "Now I wish she *would've* been hexed. I worked hard on that meal!"

"And that would explain why nothing happened to her," Kathy said.

"Maybe we should leave her frozen."

"Sam, we can't do *that*," Kathy said. "Besides, how would we explain her to Mr. Marsden once we cast the spell on him?"

Samantha shrugged. "I guess you're right."

"Okay, now let's go back across the room." Kathy led her sister back around the table, but pointed at Steven. "No, you stay where you are. I have him frozen. After we cast the spell to get him down, I don't know if my magic is going to wear off, though. So I need you to stand under him and…catch him. Or something."

Steven's eyes grew wide and he looked between Mr. Marsden and Kathy. "Are you joking? I couldn't lift him even without him being stuck to the ceiling! He probably has fifty pounds on me!"

"Be nice," Samantha scolded. "Probably only thirty-five.

His wife on the other hand…"

"Sam!" Kathy scolded.

"Still," Steven said, his eyes still wide.

"Just try," Kathy told him. "I'll try to be quick and freeze him again if it looks like he's going to squish you."

Steven grumbled, but walked around the table beneath their houseguest. "You better be quick."

"You'll be fine," Samantha assured him. Then, quietly to her sister, she added, "Hopefully."

The two sisters huddled together and began to recite the spell that Samantha had written.

Through an accident, this magic create,
Safely make Mr. Marsden deflate.

As the spell took hold, Kathy's freeze was released and Mr. Marsden sunk to the floor. It wasn't a quick fall, but one that was fast enough for Steven to rush to the man's side and help keep him upright.

"Whoa, easy there!" Steven said to him with a smile.

"What's going on?" he asked.

Samantha nudged her sister and nodded to Lucille. With a quick flick of her hand, Kathy unfroze her as well.

"Honey!" Lucille shrieked when she saw Steven helping her husband off the floor. "What happened!"

"I—I don't know. That was…this was…"

Hex

Instinctively, the Marsdens turned to Samantha for an explanation. The older witch's mind went blank at the demand for some kind of answer.

CHAPTER 10

U h…um…" Samantha stammered for the second time that evening. How was she going to explain this away? The Marsdens had seen too much. They had *experienced* too much. Mr. Marsden was literally up on the ceiling. Lucille saw everything! And how were they supposed to explain the passage of time? Surely, the Marsdens would notice that, even if Samantha could come up with a believable excuse as to what Mr. Marsden was doing up on the ceiling.

From behind her, Kathy began reciting an incantation:

To our guests, this evening is in question,
Open their minds, free them to suggestion.

HEX

Samantha spun around on her sister. "No more magic! That's the *last* thing we need after a night like this!"

"It's okay," Kathy said. "This spell only leaves them open to *suggestion*—meaning that they'll believe anything we tell them. And to make it even more believable, you could use your persuasion power to give the spell an added boost."

"Where did you find this spell?"

"I came up with it while I was making the potions," Kathy said.

"Oh, so it's *fully* foolproof."

"It's a good spell, Sam."

Samantha looked between the two Marsdens, who were both staring with blank expressions. She was hesitant to try Kathy's idea on her boss and his wife. But then again, the spell had already been cast, so the deed had already been started. Better to finish it and make sure it worked properly before someone else took advantage of their open mindset. Besides, hadn't they already been exposed to magic tonight? What was a little bit more?

"So I just…talk to them?" Samantha quietly asked her sister.

Kathy shrugged. "I guess."

"You *guess*?"

"Just give them a summary of the evening!"

"You know, this makes me wonder just how many dinner dates like this we had before we got married," Steven added. "How many spells were cast on me and my memory."

"Hush," Samantha said. "We don't have time to get into all of that."

"There weren't any that I can remember," Kathy told him. "And Sam would've called me if something like this happened with you. I think you're safe."

Steven nodded, accepting that answer.

"Okay, here it goes," Samantha said with a sigh. "Mr. Marsden…Lucille. You two had a great time tonight."

Finally, the Marsdens reacted to something. They both smiled and nodded, although their eyes were still vacant.

"You had a wonderful meal, drank a little too much wine, and when we moved to the couch to chitchat some more, you both fell asleep," she went on.

"Oh, good one," Kathy injected quietly.

"In fact," Samantha took their arms and began to lead them to the living room, "what I just told you is all that you remember about the evening." She got them in front of the couch and eased them down onto the cushions.

Kathy and Steven followed behind and sat when Samantha waved for them to do so. They each reclined, getting comfortable as if they had been sitting there for a while.

"You won't remember any of the magic you saw—floating to the ceiling, Kathy and I talking about the magic book, Kathy's beak—"

Steven snickered, but Kathy put a finger to her recently-restored lips.

"None of it will remain in your memory," Samantha finished. She turned to Kathy. "Now what?"

"Um…" Kathy thought for a moment, then snapped her fingers.

The Marsdens both jerked their heads as they were jolted out of the spell.

"That's it?" Samantha murmured.

"I guess so," Kathy said, equally impressed.

"Samantha." Mr. Marsden pushed against the arm of the couch to get to his feet. "I'm sorry, but I think I might have dosed off for a bit."

"I must've fallen asleep too," Lucille said, stifling a yawn. "How terribly rude of us. It must've been the wonderful meal you served us. It was delicious."

A wonderful meal that you pretended to eat, Samantha thought to herself, but kept the comment in her own head.

Samantha smiled. "It's no problem. I'm glad you enjoyed the dinner."

"Absolutely! Thank you for inviting us!" Mr. Marsden turned to the door and stood by for his wife to go in front of him. "We should be getting home. The dogs need to go out and we're clearly both tired." He chuckled, but it faded off in confusion.

Lucille reached for her coat and began to pull it on. "Thanks again for having us. It was so nice to finally meet you. I hear so much about how great you are at the office."

That made Samantha blush. She was about to make a comment in modesty, but Kathy nudged her from behind. Samantha turned to look and saw Kathy rubbing her fingers together, indicating money. Quickly, Samantha shook her head as the Marsdens were bundling up to head out into the cold weather.

"Thank you so much," Mr. Marsden repeated at the door. "We had a terrific time. Have a great weekend! I'll see you on Monday."

"See you Monday," Samantha called after him as he and his wife descended the front steps and walked back to their car.

After she closed the door, she turned and saw both Kathy and Steven looking at her.

"What the heck, Sam!" Kathy nearly shouted.

"What?" she asked.

"Why didn't you ask about the raise?" Kathy asked. "You had the perfect opportunity! And they might've still been open to suggestion!"

"Exactly. It was an opportunity that had been created by magic. It didn't seem fair. I want Mr. Marsden to give me a raise on his own. Not because I influenced his decision."

"I think you made the right move." Steven stepped forward to kiss his wife.

"Thanks," she muttered to him before turning back to her sister. "Besides, it's not like I'm not living on a livable wage right now. We live a comfortable life. Sure, I could use more money, but for the time being it works. Maybe when the baby comes I can try again."

"I think you should try sooner than later," Kathy said.

"Well, either way, it's not like this evening was a total loss," Samantha added. "I got to fix another magical crisis with you before you go and move out. I'm going to miss that." She put her arm around her sister and hugged her.

"The magical crises or me?"

"Hmm…I wonder which one?"

Kathy laughed. "Hey, you know something? That talisman must've worked! You left the dining room!"

Samantha pulled the talisman from her chest and examined it. "I guess it did. Do you think I'll ever be able to take it off?"

"You should, now that it's broken whatever odd magic had been put on you," Kathy said. "Everything is back to normal. Well, except the kitchen. I'm going to go start to clean up that mess."

When Kathy disappeared into the kitchen, Steven turned to Samantha and asked, "So it was a weird night?"

"You have no idea."

"I really don't," he said. "Are you going to fill me in?"

Samantha laughed. "Maybe tomorrow. I'm exhausted!"

FROM THE AUTHOR OF THE UNDER THE MOON SERIES
DAVID NETH
Don't let your guard down.
DEM8N
COVEN: BOOK 10.5

CHAPTER 1

- JANUARY 1990 -

The thumping music brought back memories for Kathy. It had been a while since she had been to the club. In the last year or so, she had "graduated" to bars, which seemed to cater to an older population. A more mature population, Kathy liked to think. But one that still liked to have fun.

Tonight, however, had not been Kathy's idea. Her original plan was to have tea with Samantha's neighbor, Mrs. Kors. However, her son had just died and their sweet neighbor was understandably not in the mood for company. Besides, Kathy had been there when Dennis had died—a fact that Mrs. Kors was unaware of. Kathy couldn't imagine trying to make small talk without that elephant in the room coming to light.

"We're going to have so much fun," Trisha said from beside

DEMON

Kathy. They had already checked their coats at the door and entered the dark and moody room.

The space was packed with people dancing, writhing up against one another. The drinks were in full swing, many of the dancers raised their plastic cups up over their heads as they swung their hips to the heavily remixed music.

Kathy grabbed at her elbows with her hands, feeling a little chilly in her black skirt. It had been a while since she had dug out that part of her closet. Her "going out" dresses had almost been donated when she had gotten her own apartment. Thankfully, she had decided to keep most of them.

"Come on," Trisha said loudly to Kathy over the sound of the music. "Let's get a drink and then we can scope out the guys."

"I'm not here to meet anyone," Kathy reminded her friend, but Trisha pulled her along without a response.

When they got to the bar, Trisha ordered them both their usual cocktails. As they waited, Kathy leaned in to her friend and said, "Don't get any ideas about me meeting anyone."

"Just relax and have fun," Trisha told her. "Whatever's going to happen will happen. Just don't get in the way."

"I'm not looking for a relationship."

"Never said you were. I respect your choice to live the single life."

"Then why are you so insistent on me meeting someone?"

"Sex, Kathy."

The witch could feel her cheeks flush. "Oh."

The bartender set their drinks on the bar and Trisha handed over her license and credit card to start her tab.

"Unless you've given up that as well?" Trisha teased as she waited for the bartender to run her card.

Kathy swallowed. "Um. No. I haven't."

The bartender brought back Trisha's credit card and she slipped it in her bra. "Good. Now let's see who we've got here."

With drinks in hand, the women turned to the crowd. Trisha sipped from her straw and grinned at all the men her eyes laid on.

"Look, Trisha, I'm not so sure about this," Kathy said.

Her friend glared at her and then set her drink on the bar, carefully placing her hand over it as she spoke. "Okay, let's have a quick chat about this. Like I said, I respect your decision to be single. But that doesn't mean you need to be such a wet blanket about everything. I mean, come on, Kathy! Loosen up and have some fun! You can stick to your pact and still have a good time."

Kathy shrugged and nodded. "That's true."

Turning back to the bar, Trisha got the bartender's attention and then ordered them shots.

Before they downed them, they clinked glasses and Trisha said, "Here's to letting loose!"

It didn't take long before Kathy started feeling the effects of the drinks that Trisha had ordered for them.

"Another?" Trisha asked. "Let's see if we can get a guy to buy us the next round!"

Kathy shook her head. "I'd better not. I want to have a good night *and* a good morning."

Trisha rolled her eyes, but smiled. "I suppose that's best. Now that we've had our liquid courage, let's get out there and have some fun!"

Taking her friend by the hand, Trisha led her onto the dance floor, where they started dancing to the music. They laughed and swayed like no one else was around.

Their jovial banter attracted the interest of guys on the prowl. The first few men who tried to cut in were immediately pushed away by Kathy. Finally, after she turned the third away, Trisha stopped and leaned in close to Kathy's ear.

"Relax. Dancing with a guy doesn't mean you need to go home with him."

Kathy nodded. She didn't used to be this uptight. Samantha must've been rubbing off on her.

So with the next man who caught her eye and gave the signals that he was interested in her, she danced with and tossed away all of the nerves she had about the evening.

The guy wasn't really even her type. He was certainly too polished—perfectly quaffed hair, a shirt that fit a little too tight, and hands softer than hers—but in the moment it didn't matter. It was just a song. Just a dance. Just one night.

Just a kiss.

As the song neared the end, she felt his lips on hers. It took a second for her to register what was happening. When it finally did, her first reaction was to pull away. But instead, she leaned into it. This was as far as it would go and she was only having fun. Trisha kissed guys all the time and she only went home with a select few of them. Dated far fewer than those, even. Maybe Kathy should take up the same model.

She finally pulled away when the song ended. Both her and the guy—what was his name?—laughed and smiled at each other, then Kathy turned to tell Trisha what had just happened.

But Trisha was gone.

Kathy pushed through the crowd toward the bathrooms and scanned the line of women waiting for their chance to use it. Trisha wasn't among them. Besides, she usually told Kathy when she was going off to the bathroom so they could talk while they waited.

Next, Kathy searched the bar. Nothing. As Kathy started making her way around the perimeter of the club, her facial expression warded off any potential advances from the guys there. She was on a mission.

Finally, with heart racing, Kathy spotted Trisha in the lounge area at the back of the club. She was pressed against the wall in a full lip-lock with a random guy. Not that Kathy was one to judge after what she herself just did.

Kathy smiled and began to move away, but then something strange happened. The guy Trisha was kissing collapsed to the floor. His body dropped like a deflated balloon.

She watched as he fell, but then her eyes shot right back up to her friend to make sure she was okay. Only, in the split second between his fall and Trisha regaining her composure, Kathy could see her friend's eyes flicker black.

CHAPTER 2

Trisha blinked and her eyes returned to her normal blue, which made Kathy blink her own eyes. Had she just imagined that?

Rushing up to Trisha, Kathy asked, "Are you okay?"

"I'm fine." Trisha looked down at the man on the floor and grabbed his arm to turn him over. "Not sure about him, though."

Kathy knelt down next to him to help her friend get him up on his feet. He was starting to regain consciousness again. "We need to call for help."

"I think he just drank too much," Trisha murmured.

The two women heaved him up to his feet and swung his arms around each of their shoulders. By time they stumbled to the edge of the lounge area, another person from the club had notified security, who took the brunt of the man's weight.

"What the hell happened to him?" the man asked.

"He just passed out," Trisha said.

"Is he with you?"

"Um…not really," Trisha told him.

"We'll take care of him," Kathy added as they came closer to the door.

The entryway was packed with people waiting to get in, checking their coats, or waiting for friends to meet up with them. The freezing winter air drifted in every time the door opened with a new group of people.

Since the security officer had taken the brunt of the work carrying the man, Kathy retrieved her and Trisha's coats from coatcheck and then rushed outside.

The man was coming to as Kathy pulled on her coat and passed Trisha hers.

"If you ladies are with him, I'm afraid I'm going to have to ask you to leave as well," the security officer said. "Do you need me to call you a cab?"

"No, we can get it," Kathy told him. "Thank you."

"No problem." Security looked to the man, who propped himself against the side of the building, pushing against his knees to keep upright. "You all right, my man?"

"Where am I?" the man asked. "What's going on?"

"We've got it," Kathy told Security. "Thanks again."

Security disappeared inside and Kathy propped up against the building next to the man.

"Are you cold?" she asked. "Did you bring a coat? We can get it if you'd like."

"I don't know," the man said.

Trisha knelt in front of him, pressing her legs together to keep her bare legs warm. "What's your name?"

Kathy noted that Trisha didn't know his name anymore than Kathy knew the name of the guy she had been kissing on the dance floor. Someone she would never see again in her life.

He thought about Trisha's question for a moment. "Uh…Hank."

"I'm Trisha and this is Kathy. Do you remember your address so we can call you a cab?"

"Trisha, he can't go home by himself," Kathy told her friend.

"I'm not ready to leave, though."

Kathy sighed. "Fine. I'll take him home, then."

Trisha raised her eyebrows, but offered nothing else. Still, Kathy could tell what she was thinking.

"Just to make sure he gets home safe," Kathy added. She turned back to Hank. "So…do you remember your address?"

Hank nodded. "Yeah, it's 711 Vine Street."

Trisha stood up straight. "Perfect. I'll go flag down a cab."

Kathy knew there would likely be at least one circling the block. This was about the only nightlife spot in the city, so it was ripe for the cab business to make a good profit every weekend.

DEMON

While Trisha was gone, Kathy rubbed Hank's back to try to comfort him. "Are you sure you're okay?"

"I don't know. I'm getting there, I think. I'm just so tired."

"Do you know what happened?"

"I don't even know how I got here."

That concerned her. It was easy to forget just what kind of dangers lurked from going out in a crowded place and letting your guard down. Kathy certainly hadn't been as careful as she usually was. Maybe somebody put something in Hank's drink that made him pass out. Kathy supposed it could happen to men just as much as it could a woman.

"What's the last thing you remember?" she asked.

"Um…being at work and getting up to use the restroom."

Kathy scrunched her eyebrows together. "Really? That's it?"

"I mean, there are bits and pieces since then that I remember, but I can't exactly remember why I was in those places." He shook his head again and buried his face in his hands. "I'm sorry. I'm just completely wiped. Maybe after a good night's sleep I'll remember more. I hope I will."

She could see his hands shaking and knew that it likely didn't have anything to do with the cold. With no other comfort to offer him, Kathy sat there and rubbed his back.

"Kathy!" Trisha called from the curb. She stood beside a cab with the rear door open. "Hurry up! Before someone takes it!"

"Come on." Kathy hooked an arm under Hank's to help lift

him, but he rose to his feet on his own. Still, she kept her place beside him to steady him.

Hank climbed into the back seat with little assistance and Kathy stood with one leg inside. She turned to Trisha. "Come with us to make sure he gets settled in. With what happened to him, I don't like the idea of you being here by yourself."

"I won't be by myself," Trisha said. "I'm meeting Doug."

"Doug?"

"We've sort of been seeing each other. It's still pretty new. Met him a couple weeks ago. But he's sweet."

"So you don't actually know him."

"He's a nice guy!" Trisha backed up toward the club entrance. "I'll be fine."

"Be careful!" Kathy called, knowing it was out of her hands. She hated watching her friend disappear back into the crowd. Especially when something happened to the grown man she was climbing into the cab with.

Not to mention whatever the hell happened to Trisha that made her eyes go black.

CHAPTER 3

Kathy set the takeout container on the counter at Trisha's apartment. It was just subs from the deli around the corner from Kathy's place.

"Thanks for getting those." Trisha opened the fridge and pulled out a pitcher of water. "Do you want anything for mine?"

Kathy waved it off. "No, it's okay. You got mine last time."

Truth be told, Kathy would've rather spent the money elsewhere. Like, perhaps, toward one of her utility bills, but Trisha *had* paid for her lunch last time. And her drinks the night before. Besides, getting together for lunch was Kathy's idea. She wanted to get more information about what happened between Trisha and Hank at the club.

Trisha filled two glasses with water and slid one to Kathy,

who had perched herself on the barstool at the breakfast bar.

"So did you have your way with that guy last night?" Trisha pulled out some napkins and set them on the breakfast bar as well. As she came around to take the seat beside her friend, she offered her a wry grin.

"Hank," Kathy clarified. "And no. He was basically asleep before we even got to his house." She unwrapped her sub and reached for a napkin.

"That's a buzzkill. He was perfectly fine when I caught his eye. But then he got really weird really fast."

"Something wasn't right about that whole thing. I'm just glad I got him home safely." She took a bite of her sandwich.

"And you're telling me that you were in a man's house alone and nothing happened between the two of you?"

Kathy finished her bite. "He was asleep, Trish. I had to help him in the door. I was lucky enough just to get him to the couch. Once I knew he was okay, I got him a glass of water, covered him with a blanket, and then left. He was out the whole time."

"Hmm. Makes you wonder if he was roofied." Trisha took another bite of her sandwich.

"You said he was fine when you were dancing with him?"

Trisha nodded, still chewing. She swallowed, then added, "We had a real connection. Obviously, I don't just kiss random people."

At that, Kathy shot her a look.

"Not *anymore*," Trisha clarified. "Anyway, one minute we

were kissing, the next he was down on the floor unconscious."

"Must've been the kiss of death." Kathy smiled to show she was joking. As she considered what else to ask about Hank, something caught her eye. At the edge of the counter, tucked along the wall, was a stack of papers. Newspapers, letters from insurance companies, circular flyers. Kathy found that she had been accumulating her own pile even in the short time that she'd lived at her apartment.

What grabbed her attention, though, was the headline on a short article of the newspaper on top: FIGHT BREAKS OUT AT NIGHTCLUB

"Is this paper current?" she asked, pulling it closer for inspection.

"Yeah," Trisha said around a mouthful. "Just came in this morning. Haven't had a chance to read it yet."

Kathy pulled it in front of her and straightened out the paper so she could read the full article. "Did you see this?"

"Hmm? The fight?"

"Yeah."

"It was kind of hard to miss."

Kathy wondered why Trisha hadn't told her about it. Here, Kathy was hooked on Hank collapsing as the weirdest thing that happened last night. But a major fight was certainly more newsworthy. And yet Trisha had been quiet about it.

"When I left everyone seemed to be having a good time," Kathy said. "What happened?"

Trisha shrugged and finished the last bite of her sandwich. Kathy patiently waited. When she was done, Trisha simply said, "Some guys get very possessive very quick."

"What do you mean?"

"Honey, they were fighting over me! Sheesh, I had to leave the club just to get them to stop."

Kathy stared at the article, trying to collect her thoughts. *Why hadn't Trisha mentioned it?* she wondered to herself.

"Anyway, how's Samantha and the baby?" Trisha asked. "You didn't really talk about them much last night."

"Oh, they're good. I mean, Josh still just sleeps a lot. But he's so cute! I swear, he recognizes my voice. Smiles every time he hears it. I can't wait to get some pictures developed. I used a whole roll on him!"

Trisha smiled. "So you see him a lot?"

"Almost every day. I mean, he's only a week old, but I just can't get enough of him. Actually, besides going to work, last night was probably the most 'adult' thing I've done in a while."

"Well, as happy as I am for your sister, I'm glad you're still just 'auntie' so that we can still hang out."

"Yeah," Kathy mused. "Honestly, I should probably be giving them more space than I have been. Steven has started giving me those looks, you know? Like he's annoyed that I'm there."

Just before Kathy had gone out with Trisha the night before, Steven had asked her, "I thought you moved out?" It was an innocent enough comment, made in humor, but Kathy could sense the intentions behind his words.

"I think we can take care of that." Trisha waved her hand to the newspaper and Kathy handed it to her. Trisha flipped it open and said, "You want to see a movie? Let's see what they're playing."

"Sounds good to me."

CHAPTER 4

Kathy and Trisha arrived at the movie theater just before the previews started playing. Trisha had splurged on popcorn, but Kathy refrained. The movie ticket was expensive enough. Five dollars just to see a movie? That was a little steep for only a couple hours of entertainment. Especially when she had her electric bill to think about.

The theater was crowded and they had to squeeze around outstretched legs in between the rows to find two seats next to each other that hadn't been taken.

"I'm excited," Trisha said as she settled in her seat.

Kathy peeled off her coat and draped it over her legs. "Me too! I've been waiting for this movie since the first one came out."

Demon

They had decided on *Back to the Future Part II*. It had just come out two months ago and Kathy had heard that it was good.

"I know! Michael J. Fox could find me in *any* time period and I'd be okay with that." Trisha laughed and Kathy soon joined in.

Behind them, someone rudely said, "Shh!" so they both quieted and watched the rest of the previews.

The movie started, picking up right where the first one had left off. Kathy wished she had watched the first one on video before seeing the second one, but she hadn't expected to see a movie.

As Marty McFly and Doc traveled to the future, Kathy found herself envisioning just what the year 2015 would be like. She'd be 48 then! And little baby Josh would be almost 26, older than Kathy was now.

As she watched, something caught Kathy's attention that drew her away from the movie. Up ahead one row to the right, she noticed a man suddenly sit upright in his seat. The man behind him, huffed and put his feet up on the back of his chair. It was only for a few seconds before he sat up straighter and tried to see around the first guy.

In Kathy's gut, she could sense that something bad was about to happen. There was a shift in the atmosphere that didn't sit right with her. It wasn't concrete evidence to go off of, just a feeling, but that feeling had never steered Kathy wrong before.

Before she could put her finger on what exactly was brewing

just under the surface, the guy in the second row leaned up to the guy in the first row and whispered something in his ear.

Whatever it was, Kathy couldn't hear over the sound of the movie. But it got the guy in the front row riled up enough that he stood and began shouting at the guy behind him.

"What the hell do you expect me to do about my height, huh? I can't help how tall I am, but you could've found somewhere else to sit."

"Nah, no matter where I sat I wouldn't be able to see around that fat head of yours," Second Row fired back. "Besides, you could have a little courtesy for the rest of us and take a seat in the back row. It's not like this tall thing is new for you."

"No, but dealing with assholes like you is," First Row said.

In response, Second Row punched First Row right in the jaw and sent him flying back over the seats in front of him. Second Row leapt over the seats to chase after him.

"Oh my God!" someone shouted.

Another person shot up to their feet and ran out of the theater to get help.

Soon, the movie stopped and the lights came on. Everyone else in the theater stopped and looked around, not sure what to do. Some people joined in on the brawl. Others ran out of the theater in a panic.

Kathy and Trisha were among those who stayed. Trisha, because she was frozen to her seat, and Kathy, because she wanted to be there in case things got really bad. Still, it wasn't like she could freeze the room. There were too many people and they were all coming and going.

Security raced in and started breaking up the brawl. Additional guards ushered the crowd to empty the theater. With no other choice, Kathy and Trisha followed suit and exited. Kathy reasoned with herself that at least this wasn't a magical attack. Two men fighting in a theater was entirely within the security guards' abilities to handle on their own.

"I've never known a theater to stop a movie mid-showing," Kathy said when they were back out in the winter gloom. She shielded her eyes against the brightness, even with the cloud cover.

Trisha shrugged. "I guess this was just a weird circumstance."

"That really was weird." They crossed the street to where Trisha had parked on the other side. "I mean, it's annoying to sit behind someone you can't see around. But to punch them for it and get in a fight?"

Trisha unlocked her door with the key and shrugged again. "People are crazy!"

CHAPTER 5

When Kathy woke up the next day on Sunday, she had a terrible feeling in the pit of her stomach. All night long she had had the strangest dreams. Ones that felt more like reality than unconscious fiction.

She got up and visited the bathroom before making her way into the kitchen to pour her breakfast into a bowl. She used up the last of the milk and frowned. Payday wasn't until Friday, which meant that she would have to go a whole week with dry cereal.

As she sat down at the counter to eat, she recalled her dreams. In every one, no matter the variations that led up to that moment, she clearly saw Trisha's eyes turn black for a second. The more she thought it over, the stronger the memory became and the more Kathy realized it hadn't been a dream at all, but something she had witnessed Friday night in the club. At the time, she had brushed it off as her drunken mind playing tricks on her. But she hadn't been *that* drunk and so she was starting to believe that the memory could be trusted.

But what did it mean?

Kathy had been with Trisha the whole night. The only time they had separated was when Kathy had been dancing with that guy and Trisha went off with Hank.

Maybe that was the connection. Not only did something weird happen to Trisha, but Hank collapsed out of nowhere too. And both instances happened right after the two of them kissed.

Kathy got up from her seat and rinsed her bowl. She tried to put the thoughts out of her mind. Sure, what had happened at the club was weird, but she had spent most of Saturday with Trisha and she seemed fine. And Hank seemed fine Friday night when Kathy took him back to his house. Obviously, he was tired, but who wasn't at one in the morning?

After going for a quick run, she showered and went upstairs to pick out her clothes for work for the week. With her wardrobe decided, Kathy came back downstairs and dug through her pile of library books. She chose one that had been sitting on her kitchen counter for a week.

Taking a seat on the couch, she tried to get into the book. Reading was something she always loved to do, but it had become her only option for entertainment since moving out on her own. Between the rent and the utilities, the monthly costs were steeper than Kathy had realized they would be. Luxury items like cable had to be put off. So she found herself stopping at the library more to get a collection of books. It was amazing how much she could read without the distraction of TV.

Kathy made it to page four before she realized she hadn't been paying attention to a single thing she had been reading. Her thoughts were too preoccupied with Trisha and Hank.

Closing the book, she got up and reached for her coat. She needed to consult the magic book and maybe even Samantha about it. She wasn't convinced that what had happened was magical, but at least it would rule out an option in her mind and start her on the path to explaining things.

She made it to the street before she had second thoughts about going back home. Samantha was probably overwhelmed with the baby. The last thing she needed was to worry about something that might actually be nothing.

But Kathy couldn't just sit by and ignore what had happened. Especially when it happened to one of her closest friends, and a sweet guy like Hank.

That was it. She knew where Hank lived. She could go visit him and get *his* version of the story now that he had had a day to recover and think about it.

Kathy took the bus down to the stop nearest Hank's house. He actually didn't live too far from her. If the weather hadn't been so cold, she probably would've walked. Bus fare, and all.

DEMON

Hank's house was the only yellow one on the short little street. She knocked on the door, eyeing up the houses nearby. Friday night when she had dropped him off, she hadn't picked up on the fact that the area wasn't the greatest. Certainly far from the worst in the city, but these houses required a level of love and care that out-of-state landlords refused to give them.

Which is why she was grateful when Hank opened the door and immediately invited her in.

Kathy kicked off the snow from her boots on the mat just inside the door.

"Do you want anything to drink?" Hank asked as he moved into the small kitchen off the entry hallway. He acted as if he had been expecting her.

Kathy kicked off her boots and hung her coat by the door. "Something warm if you have it."

"Coffee or tea?"

"What kind of tea do you have?" She joined him in the kitchen.

"Lemon tea okay?"

"Sounds good to me."

The kitchen was tiny. Clearly haphazardly modernized to fit a fridge, stove, and microwave all in the tight space. There was only a small stretch of countertop between the sink and the microwave to prepare any food, although she had her doubts Hank did much cooking.

Kathy took a seat at the small bistro table by the window. It was metal and uncomfortable, but she couldn't stand the idea of standing around idly while Hank prepared her tea. That would make the situation more awkward than it already was.

Hank set the teapot on the stove to boil and then turned and leaned against the counter. He wore a hooded sweatshirt with the Gannon University logo on it and plain gray sweatpants.

"How have you been feeling?" Kathy asked.

He shrugged. "Not bad, actually."

"So your memory's back?"

"I remembered you." He offered her a smile. "Thanks for helping me home the other night. I doubt I would've made it here on my own if it hadn't been for you."

"Of course. I wasn't going to just leave you there."

Hank turned and grabbed two mugs from the cupboard. "Well, a lot of people would have."

Kathy thought of Trisha, who just wanted to put Hank in a cab and then go back into the club and party. That was another one of her strange behaviors. As wild as Trisha could be, she was always very careful when she went out to the club. She knew the dangers and she was prepared for them.

"Do you have any idea why you just collapsed?"

He shook his head as he turned off the burner to silence the whistling teapot. "No. And what's weirder is that I don't seem to remember the last week, even. And I'm still exhausted." He dunked the teabags into the mugs and carried one over to

Kathy. "Actually, do you mind if we go sit in the living room? I just—I need to sit down."

"Oh sure. Do you want me to carry that for you?" She indicated his tea.

"No, I've got it. Thank you, though." He led her across the entry hallway into the front living room.

Just like the kitchen, it was small. The furniture was too big for the space. The rug had a dingy color to it, although it looked fairly clean besides that.

"This is nice." Kathy took a seat at the end of the couch since there was no other place to sit.

"It's really not," he said as he took the spot on the other end. "My friend and I moved in here when we were in college. He moved out last summer and I've been stuck with the lease. Can't break it until it's up in June. Then I'm out of here."

"At least you have the place to yourself," she said.

"Yeah." He took a careful sip of his tea and set it on the table beside the couch. "So do you want to talk about what you're really here for? Actually, could you start with your name?" He chuckled. "I never got that. I'm Hank, in case I didn't tell you that."

She smiled and wrapped her cold hands around the hot mug. "You did. I'm Kathy. And I guess I just wanted to check in on you. I felt kind of bad just leaving you here Friday, but I figured it was better than you waking up to some random lady in your house."

He laughed. "Yeah, that would've been weird, but on track with the rest of the night."

"Did any other weird things happen to you that night?"

"Honestly, I don't remember. Like I said, I'm having a hard time remembering the last week."

"Friday you said that the last thing you remembered was being at work."

He nodded. "Yep. I think it was last Tuesday, maybe. Everything was fine. I went to use the bathroom at work, but as soon as I got inside someone jumped me. Grabbed me from behind. The next thing I remember, I was waking up on the floor of the club."

"You don't remember anything else?"

Hank let out a deep breath as he thought about it. "Just bits and pieces. Like, I remember leaving work, but it's kind of wrapped in a fog. I remember being super annoyed at the traffic that day. And I remember coming home, but that's about it. Honestly, anything after that is a complete blur until Friday night when you helped me home."

"Hmm." Kathy thought about it. Trisha mentioned a roofie, but that certainly wouldn't last all week. This *had* to be magical, but how? "Do you know who it was who jumped you?"

"Not at all. Didn't get a look at his face. I don't think he had a weapon or anything. He just grabbed me from behind and then..." He shrugged. "I don't think anything...*bad* happened. Not like—"

Kathy shook her head. "No, that's not what I was thinking either. I'm just trying to make sense of it all."

Hank let out a humorless laugh. "Join the club."

"I'm going ask you a really strange question, so keep an open mind."

He smiled at her. "This has never been a stranger time in my life, so now's the time to ask."

"In the bits and pieces that you *do* remember from the last week, do you recall any fights that happened around you?"

He started to shake his head no, but stopped. "Not vividly. I think I might've punched someone. And I'm only saying that because my hand has been sore all weekend."

"Oh okay." Kathy nodded, a little disappointed. Hank *might've* gotten in a fight, but she can't rely on his answer.

"I do remember just being angry all the time. I think that's part of the reason I'm so tired. The anger was just constant. It put so much stress on my body that I'm wiped."

"Angry about what?"

He shrugged. "Nothing in particular stands out."

"Interesting," she muttered.

Hank yawned.

"I should let you get some rest." She stood and waved her empty tea cup toward the kitchen. "I can set this in the sink if you want."

"That would be great, thanks."

Kathy threw the teabag in the trash and then rinsed out her

mug. On an envelope on the counter, she wrote down her name and number.

"Hank, I'm leaving you my number in case…" She trailed off when she returned to the living room and saw that he had fallen asleep. Back in the kitchen, she wrote on the envelope beneath her number: "If you remember anything or need anything, give me a call. Feel better!"

As she put on her boots, she gave one last look in Hank's direction and then walked out the door.

CHAPTER 6

Kathy could hear the sound of baby Josh crying before she even stepped foot in the house. When she got inside the Victorian home, she saw Samantha pacing around the living room with her wailing infant on her shoulder. His little face was a deep red as he made his displeasure known.

"Oh! Look Josh! Aunt Kathy is here!" Samantha cooed when she saw her sister.

Kathy could see dark circles under her sister's eyes. As she stepped into the foyer, she saw Steven half-asleep on a chair. His feet were propped up on the coffee table. His shirt was wrinkled and had a small white spit-up stain near the left shoulder.

"Can you take him for a bit?" Samantha asked. "I just need to lie down."

"Gimme that baby!" Kathy cheered. As she took her nephew in her arms and held him close to her, she turned on her baby voice and asked, "What's the matter, Josh? It's okay. Aunt Kathy is here. Your parents are just a little tired. It's okay if you need a break too."

Samantha lay back on the couch, not even questioning Kathy's arrival. Since Josh had been born, her presence had been pretty consistent.

"I'm just here to borrow the magic book," Kathy said to Josh, still in the baby voice.

"For what?" Samantha asked.

"Nothing crazy," Kathy said, trying to spare her sister the stress. "I just miss flipping through it and staying up-to-date in all things witchcraft."

"That sounds like a line, but I'm too tired to question it," Samantha said.

"If there's evil around, don't bring it here," Steven added. "We already have one demon, no need for another."

"Steven!" Samantha snapped. "Don't call our son that. He's a baby. He cries."

"Well, it would be nice if he stopped once and a while."

"Figure out what he wants and he will."

"Guys," Kathy cut in. "None of this is helping anyone. Josh can tell you're both stressed out and you're saying things you don't mean. Let me take care of him for a bit and you guys can take a nap."

Samantha shook her head and sat up. "No. I can do it. I have to pump anyway."

"Then you go do that and let me spend some time with my nephew. Maybe I can get him to sleep and then you can take a nap. Everyone here just needs some sleep." Even Kathy could feel her patience waning thin as Josh continued to wail in her ear. "Could he be hungry?"

"I tried that," Samantha said. "He wouldn't take it. From me or the bottle."

"Diaper?"

"Changed it," Steven said.

Kathy looked around the room and noted how quickly their regal, historic living room had become Baby Central in the matter of a week. "Let me see his pacifier." She shifted Josh so she was cradling him.

"He wouldn't take it," Steven said. "I tried."

Samantha passed it to her sister anyway.

Kathy stuck the pacifier in Josh's mouth, which muffled his screams. She held it in place until he realized that it was there and began sucking on it. Soon, his screaming subsided and after a minute, his breathing settled too.

"You did it!" Samantha cheered quietly. She leaned forward and kissed Josh's forehead and then did the same to Kathy's. "Oh my gosh, I thought I was going to lose my mind."

"I've already lost mine," Steven said with a smirk. He stretched out and settled in the chair for his own nap.

"You go take care of your breasts," Kathy told her sister. "I'll make sure he's out and then put him down."

Samantha shot her sister a look at her candor, but smiled and said, "Thank you." With a lingering look at Josh, she disappeared into the kitchen to grab her pump.

Kathy rocked Josh for a few more minutes before gently setting him in the bassinet. She hovered, anticipating the screams to resume, but they didn't. The baby lay back and sucked on his pacifier, sound asleep.

Pulling herself away from her nephew, Kathy went up and retrieved the magic book from its new hiding location: under Samantha's bed. After it had been stolen from their house last week when Samantha was in the hospital having Josh, Samantha wanted to put it in a locked safe but Kathy didn't think that was wise. Instead, they settled on keeping it in her room for a more secure location than Kathy's old, empty bedroom.

With the book in hand, Kathy passed by the foyer and waved goodbye to Samantha, who was walking out of the kitchen.

"Leaving already?"

"Yeah. I have to run."

Samantha eyed the book. "Are you sure everything's all right?"

"Everything's fine, Sam. Don't worry about me. You have enough going on right now."

"Still not putting my mind at ease. Look, if there's

something witchy we need to worry about, let me help. You seem to be the only one who can put my kid to sleep, so I kind of need you around."

Kathy smirked. "Stop worrying and just take the time to be a mom right now."

Samantha made a face. "Ooooh. Mom. That's weird."

"That's not the weirdest thing I've heard." Kathy gave her sister another hug and said, "Call me if Josh stresses you out again. You know I'm never mad about coming over to see him."

"I will. Thanks again. And be safe."

"I always am!"

CHAPTER 7

Kathy absently flipped through *The Art of Magic* back at her apartment. She was perched on the couch, her microwavable dinner steaming on the coffee table, looking as unappetizing as it smelled.

She had already been through the book twice and the closest thing she could find was a poltergeist possession. Based on her experience with Samantha's possession in the fall, she didn't think that's what had caused Trisha's eyes to go black. For one, Samantha's eyes never flickered black when she was possessed. And two, Samantha's attitude had gotten progressively worse the longer the poltergeist was inside her.

Trisha, on the other hand, seemed pretty much the same as she always had. Once again, for the millionth time, Kathy wondered if she had imagined the black eyes. But there was more to the story that was still unexplained. The numerous fights in her presence. Hank's collapse. His lack of memory.

Turning back to her dinner, she picked at it and forced herself to eat it. She would have to stop at the grocery store on her way home from work the next day. In lieu of going out with Trisha on Friday, she had given up her usual Friday evening grocery run. Maybe now was the time to learn how to cook.

Samantha had always been the cook growing up. Even before their father disappeared, that was one of the roles of mothering that she assumed long before she became a mother. It was among the reasons Kathy knew that Samantha was going to be a great mother. It was innate in her. Baby Josh was lucky, even if they were going through a learning curve.

Steven's words about Josh being a demon sprung to Kathy's mind. Not because it had been a rude thing to call an infant, but because that was one thing she hadn't looked at in the magic book yet.

Turning back to the book, she found the page on demons and read the entry:

The most basic form of demonic creature, demons lie at the bottom of the demonic hierarchy. While the term "demon" can be ambiguous, they're typically the henchmen, lackeys, and soldiers for higher-level commanding officers.

It is possible for the nonmagical to become demons and eventually develop magic themselves. This typically only happens after a nonmagical person allows themselves to be consumed with anger and hate without any mercy for the destruction they've caused.

Despite being at the bottom of the hierarchy, there have been some demons who have worked their way up to a position of power, greatly increasing the strength of their powers. Even though they're at the bottom, it's important to be wary of demons as well.

Kathy sat back, a little disappointed in what she had read. She really thought that was a possibility for a second. She started to close the book, but another thought occurred to her: wasn't there lore that demons had the capability to possess people?

Before getting too excited, her mind found reasons to reject that thought. Lore was typically passed down from generation to generation by word-of-mouth. The reliability of what was considered "lore" was automatically in question because of that.

Of course, lore existed because of someone's personal experience. Granted, that personal experience was very long ago and there could've been any number of factors that actually influenced that experience, but at least it was something.

She didn't want to rule out the possibility simply because *The Art of Magic* didn't have it. After all, their magic book was a family magic book. If something wasn't included, it simply meant that their family hadn't encountered anything like that in the past.

Armed with this new idea, Kathy reached for the phone and called Trisha.

"Hello?" her friend asked when she picked up.

"Trish? It's me, Kathy. I'm just calling to check in."

There was a brief pause and then Trisha said, "Why would you need to check in on me?"

"I don't know. Just to see how you're doing."

"I'm fine, Kathy."

"Has everything been good then?"

"I mean, my microwave shorted out on me and my dishwasher is making some weird noise, but yeah. Otherwise it's a normal Sunday night."

Did wonky appliances count as the same as everything else that had been happening in Trisha's presence? Maybe they did if there was no one else nearby.

"No more fights or anything?"

"What, do you think I'm some kind of bad luck charm or something?"

"No, of course not. Just want to make sure you're being safe."

Trisha sighed into the phone. "Lord, you're starting to sound like my mother—and I already have one of those. Yes, I'm fine. Everything around me is fine. What's bothering me is the third degree from you."

"Sorry," Kathy said. "Call me if anything comes up."

"Sure. Talk to you later." Without waiting for a goodbye, Trisha hung up.

Kathy set the phone back in its cradle. She doubted very much that Trisha would call. Especially if she was being controlled by a demon. But for the moment, she was content with the fact that everything was okay in Trisha's world. Maybe that would help Kathy sleep through the night okay. She would stop at the library tomorrow and see if she could find anything else about demons to confirm the lore that she remembered.

Maybe then she would start to get some answers.

CHAPTER 8

"What kind of demons are you interested in?" the librarian asked the next day. He was younger than Kathy had expected. She hadn't seen him working before and she wondered if he had just started or if he had transferred from another branch.

A guy who reads and is knowledgable about demons? she thought to herself. *That wouldn't be bad...*

She had just come from work, so she was dressed nicer than her usual trips to the library. She thought that maybe that would leave a good impression on him.

And then she remembered her pact to stay single and pushed the thought entirely from her mind.

"I'm not sure yet," she responded. "Just in general. What

their abilities are, their motivations, that kind of stuff."

"Well, it would depend on the mythology you look at." The man—Brian, according to the name tag on the counter in front of him—came around the desk and started leading Kathy through the stacks. "I'll show you our mythology section and maybe then we can narrow down your search from there."

"Sounds good," she murmured as she followed him.

He led her down one row of bookshelves. The endcaps were marked with numbers, which Kathy knew from school as the Dewey decimal system. She couldn't remember what each number stood for, though.

Brian, however, seemed to have the numbering sequence down pat, and he strode down the aisle, stopping nearly halfway down. His eyes scanned up and down, before he knelt and searched a shelf near the floor.

His finger traced the spines of the books. "This one is more of a pop culture account, but we also have Roman mythology, Greek mythology, and Norse mythology. I'd say those are the top three, but if you're interested in Native American stories or even lore from Asian cultures, we can find those for you too. Some of those texts might need to come from other libraries, though."

Kathy chewed on her thumb as she considered. "Could I peruse the books on the big three, and maybe the pop culture one? I can narrow it down from there."

"Sure, no problem." He pulled out the books and carried

them over to an empty table for her. "Let me know if you need help with anything else. And when you're done with these books, you can bring them right up to me."

She flashed him a smile as she set her purse in the empty seat beside her. "I will. Thanks for your help."

Equipped with the books, she pulled open the generic pop culture one and almost immediately pushed it away. Instead of recalling the traditional stories about demons, the book focused more on the entertainment adaptations of demons in movies and TV shows within the last fifteen years. She pushed it aside.

The one on Roman mythology only mentioned that demons existed, but didn't list anything beyond "fiendish acts" or "creatures who spread torment through nefarious means."

The Greek and Norse mythology books contained more or less the same type of information. She slammed each book closed, frustrated that she was coming up short.

Maybe it's not a demon, she considered. *Or maybe it's nothing at all.*

But no. It definitely *was* something. Trisha was mostly acting like herself, but the two fight outbreaks were not just coincidences. There were external forces causing them.

Stacking the books on top of each other, Kathy was about to push her chair back to ask Brian for more books when she heard someone talking suddenly behind her.

She jumped and managed to stifle a shriek in the quiet library, then breathed a sigh of relief when she saw Brian approach with a book in his hands.

His cheeks flared red. "Sorry. Didn't mean to scare you. I just wanted to show you this."

"What is it?" Kathy asked, as he set the book beside her and then leaned over the table.

"Well, I was doing a search in the database for other books we might have that would contain information about demons and I came across this. It's a book of Christian mythology, where demons are portrayed almost as the opposites of angels."

Kathy made a face. "Angels?"

Brian shrugged. "It's Christian mythology, so angels are everywhere. But what I wanted to show you was this." He pointed to a passage on the page he held open.

She skimmed it as best as she could from her seat and saw words like "wreak havoc in their wake" and "use human vessels."

"Oh," she said, her voice conveying her interest.

"Is this what you're looking for?"

"This is exactly what I'm looking for." She pulled the book closer to read it.

"It gets a bit heavy in the details, but the gist of it is that demons are like walking bad luck charms. Some need human vessels to possess in order to spread the havoc among other humans, while others are able to walk freely among us. Kind of weird to think about, right?"

Weird.

There was that word again.

DEMON

The fights that happened in Trisha's presence certainly qualified as "havoc." And maybe Hank collapsing was the demon transferring possession from Hank to Trisha. Hank wouldn't remember the time from his possession because he wasn't the one occupying his own conscious thought. The demon would've been at the time.

"Apparently most people are able to repel a demon's attempt to possess them," Brian went on. "It's when someone is impaired, such as people struggling with depression, exhaustion, or a high level of stress, that the demons are able to get the better of them and take control."

Friday night Trisha had been drunk, so that certainly counted as an impairment. Kathy knew that sometimes the lines between the natural and the supernatural were blurred when alcohol was involved. That's how she and Samantha had gotten mixed up with the valkyries a year and a half ago.

And Hank was at work when he remembered blacking out. So, Kathy wondered, maybe he was under a lot of stress and that left him susceptible. If nothing else, it was the best theory she had so far.

"Do any of these books provide ways for how to stop them?" she asked. "Like pull a demon from someone?"

"What, do you know someone who is possessed?" he joked.

She laughed nervously. "Oh, sure. Of course. I was, uh, just…wondering."

He shrugged and flipped through a few pages. "An exorcism

is my best guess. I can do some more research and get back to you."

"No, that's okay. I think I've got all that I need." She rose to her feet and gathered her things. "Thanks again for your help."

"Is there anything else you need?" Brian asked.

"No, you've already done so much."

"Uh…are you, um…" He clearly wanted her to stay, so she paused.

"Is there something wrong?" She looked at her belongings. "Did I pick up one of your books without checking it out?"

"No, that's not—I was just wondering—would you like to get coffee? My shift ends in half an hour. I could meet you at the café down on State." He pointed in the direction.

Kathy knew just what café he was talking about. She offered him a sad smile. "Look, I don't want you to take this personally, but I'm just not dating right now."

His face turned red and he looked down at the stack of books in his hand. "Oh. I see. No, it's okay. I understand."

Seeing his disappointment, she added quickly, "If I was, though, you'd definitely be the type I would be interested in."

"Really?"

She offered him a smile, even if she doubted her own words. He was cute and she liked that he was funny, but he was certainly not like any of the other guys she had dated. "Absolutely," she said.

"Thanks."

DEMON

She touched his shoulder. "Thanks again for all of your help." She nodded to the door. "I should probably go, though, before this becomes even more awkward."

Brian let out a nervous chuckle. "Yeah. Thanks for letting me down easy."

"Good luck," she said just before turning away.

"You too!" he called after her.

Thanks, she thought to herself. *I'm going to need it.*

CHAPTER 9

gain?" Trisha asked on the phone. "We just spent the whole weekend together."

Kathy was huddled in the payphone just outside the library. After what she had learned about demons possessing the nonmagical, she didn't want to wait a moment longer. Besides, Kathy was confident in her ability to use a similar exorcism spell that Clarence had used on Samantha when she had been possessed by a poltergeist.

"I know," Kathy said to her friend. She noted the bitterness in Trisha's voice. Usually she could rely on Trisha for always being down to hang out. So her reaction was yet another indicator that something was off. "But is it too much to want to spend time with one of my best friends?"

"It is when that friend could possibly get laid. I have a date tonight!"

Same old crude humor, Kathy thought to herself. A flicker of doubt crept in her mind.

With a shake of the head, Kathy cast the doubt aside. With all of the unexplained things that had happened around Trisha in the last few days, this was the only explanation.

"Trish, you always have the opportunity to get laid," Kathy said. "Don't pretend like you don't turn the heads of nearly every guy that passes."

That seemed to cheer her friend up. "Well, that's true."

"So just come over for dinner before your date," Kathy suggested. "I'll keep it light. I really only have salads in the house anyway."

"Girl, you need to go shopping!"

"It's on the list," she muttered. "So will you come? Let's be honest, it's not like you were really going out to dinner for your date, right?"

"Ha!" Trisha laughed on the other end. "You know me so well! No, we were going to go to a bar for a drink. It's a first date, so you know my rule on that."

Kathy knew that Trisha usually insisted her first dates only go out for drinks at a bar. She reasoned that if the date ended up being weird or she didn't like him for whatever reason, it was easier to end the date early at a bar than sit through an awkward dinner just to settle up the check.

"Perfect," Kathy said. "So you can come over before, right?"

Her friend sighed on the other end. "Fine. I'll be there in half an hour. But I'm leaving right at seven. That's when Peter gets out of work."

"Awesome!" Kathy cheered. "I'll see you later then. Bye!" She hung up the phone and rushed out of the phone booth toward the bus stop.

There were several places she had to stop before Trisha came over and half an hour didn't leave her a lot of time to prepare.

CHAPTER 10

Kathy was just finishing up everything she needed to get ready when Trisha arrived thirty minutes later. The first thing that Kathy noticed was how sickly her friend looked. The bags under her eyes, the pallor skin, her drab and stringy hair. The second thing she noticed was that she had made an effort to look nice. She wore a daring white dress that hugged her tight, and had added makeup to her eyes, which seemed to only make her look more tired.

What was surprising, though, was that Trisha moved as if everything were perfectly normal and that she was as well-rested as always.

"I would ask what is new, but I can pretty much guarantee that nothing is," Trisha said as a greeting when she walked in.

She set her purse on the counter—one that matched her outfit—and set one hand on her hip. "If we're going to make these get-togethers a nearly daily thing, there is just one thing I need to know from you."

Kathy was taken aback by the force that Trisha entered with, so she simply raised her eyebrows and asked, "And that is?"

"Do you have romantic feelings for me?"

In the silence that followed by Kathy's surprised, Trisha added, "I have nothing against the idea, I would just like to know what I'm getting into."

Recovering, Kathy shook her head. "No, not at all. I'm just…still adjusting to being on my own. That's all."

"Oh, that's right. You've been whining on about your sister." Trisha turned and plopped on the couch. "Oh well. It was just an idea. I thought maybe I could kill two birds with one stone tonight, but if you're not interested…"

Stunned, Kathy stared at her friend for a moment before remembering the real reason she had invited her. "Water?"

"No, dear, I'm okay."

"Are you sure? It'll help keep you hydrated for tonight's…events." Kathy had picked up holy water from a local church on her way back from the library. It was one of the key ingredients with the poltergeist exorcism, so she figured it would work with a demon too.

Obviously, she wasn't going to tell Trisha that.

"No, I said I'm fine."

Demon

Kathy brought the glass over to her and set it on the table beside her. "Just in case you change your mind."

"Are you deaf?" Trisha snapped. She reached for the glass and raised it to throw it back at Kathy, but as some of the water spilled out, it touched it her hand and she recoiled as the blessed water sizzled off of her skin. The glass fell to the floor and shattered as Trisha aimed her anger at Kathy.

"That's—" Kathy fished for an explanation, but decided there was no use in offering one.

Darting to her feet, Trisha charged to Kathy, her eyes as black as they had been Friday night.

"What the hell are you trying to do to me?" she demanded.

Instinctively, Kathy raised her hands and froze her friend. Her magic held momentarily, but shortly after the freeze took hold, Trisha began moving ever so slowly, growing faster with each passing second.

Without knowing how long her magic would last, Kathy darted up the stairs to her bedroom and retrieved the magic book from under her bed. She had bookmarked the page on exorcisms, although now that the time was upon her, her nerves were getting the better of her. Her fingers struggled to flip to the correct page.

With her nose still buried in the book, Kathy felt a hand on her shoulder. She caught the slightest glimpse of those black eyes before Trisha threw her onto her back and stood over her in that white dress. Trisha held out her hand and a ball of fire formed in her palm.

Kathy's eyes went wide at the sight of it, but before Trisha could turn the fireball on her, the witch froze the demon. This time, Kathy's magic wasn't nearly as strong as the first and instead of coming to a complete stop, the demon fought through Kathy's power, gaining speed with each passing second.

The demon was learning.

Even if Kathy hadn't fully frozen the demon and only put them in slow motion, it was still enough time for her to scramble out from under her friend and get to the trunk at the foot of the bed. That was where she stored some of the magical necessities in case the need arose.

And this was certainly a need.

Fishing out a black cord and a black candle, Kathy closed the trunk and hurried to tie the cord around Trisha's waist before she unfroze. She managed a loose knot and returned to the candle to light it.

The color black assisted in magic related to banishments, expelling negative energies, protection, and power. Clarence had used different spiritual tools when dispossessing Samantha from the poltergeist, but a vengeful spirit and a demon were two different beasts. Besides, Kathy only had herself to rely on now. She had to improvise.

Snatching the lighter, she tried to get the wick to catch, but it was a new candle and she couldn't hold the flame to it long enough before Trisha completely unfroze.

Kathy's eyes looked up just as Trisha turned to her. Casually, the demon untied the cord from around her waist and then raised her hand to Kathy. With a flick of her wrist, the demon sent the witch flying into the brick exterior wall.

The impact made Kathy's vision blur out. Her head felt as if it were about to burst. Gingerly, she reached behind her and felt the blood trickling from the back of her head. It wasn't a lot, but enough to be concerned.

After a few seconds, her vision cleared and she came to just as Trisha loomed over her with those big black eyes.

CHAPTER 11

The demon didn't wait for Kathy to get her bearings. She reached down and grabbed the witch's throat, raising her to eye level and slamming her against the wall again.

Luckily, this time Kathy was prepared enough to hold her head steady so it didn't slam against the bricks a second time. But now her vision was blurring for a different reason: she couldn't breathe.

The witch grasped at her friend's hand, trying to get her to let go. Desperate, Kathy kicked Trisha in the stomach.

The effects were immediate.

Trisha backed away, gasping for air. Kathy fell to the floor, coughing.

Apparently, even though the demon didn't need to breathe,

whatever happened to the host's body still impacted the being that possessed it. As much as Kathy hated referring to her friend as a "host," she was grateful to be equipped with that knowledge.

The reprieve didn't last long, though. Kathy used the wall to help her get to her feet as Trisha used the bedpost to do the same.

The witch, however, was quicker. She raised both hands and froze the demon where she stood. With the host—Trisha—weakened from the kick, Kathy's magic took full effect.

Kathy rushed to where the cord lay at the end of the bed and tied it around Trisha's ankles. Even if the demon were to unfreeze before the spell was complete, she'd trip and fall, giving Kathy precious seconds to finish the exorcism.

With the cord fastened around Trisha's feet, Kathy lit the black candle and held it in her hand.

Trisha unfroze and turned in place to see Kathy on the other side of the bed.

"You're all alone, witch," she taunted as she summoned another fireball. "But I don't want to kill you. All I'm going to do is weaken you enough for me to take over. Then I'll have a host strong enough to withstand my power."

Kathy had a retort, but she kept to herself. Instead, she raised the candle in the direction of her friend's body and recited the spell.

DAVID NETH

Evil spirit, I banish thee.
From now until eternity.
Release your host, set her free.
Depart from this world, let us be.

A mysterious wind picked up, circling both Kathy and Trisha. Somehow, though, the candle remained lit.

The fireball in Trisha's hand disintegrated as she staggered back, nearly tripping on the cord tied around her feet. She held her balance long enough for her face to turn skyward and a black cloud to erupt out of her mouth like a volcanic eruption.

Within seconds, the exorcism was over and Trisha collapsed forward onto Kathy's bed.

The witch stared, wide-eyed from her perch on the other end of the bed.

Did the spell work? she wondered.

Then Trisha began to stir with a groan. It was a soft, delicate whimper that Kathy knew was her friend.

Blowing out the candle, she stashed it and the magic book under the bed. Then she rounded to the other side, where she untied Trisha's ankles. Reaching for her hand, Kathy helped her sit up.

"Take a deep breath," Kathy said. "You're okay."

"Kathy?" Trisha raised a hand to her head. "What happened? My head is killing me."

"Migraine," Kathy blurted. "You asked if you could stop

over here after work to lie down. I heard you crying and thought I'd check on you."

Trisha pouted her bottom lip. "You're such a good friend." She pulled Kathy in for a hug and then a moment later she pulled away. "Wait a minute. You said I was at work?"

Kathy panicked. She should've come up with a better excuse before the exorcism, but it wasn't like she had a lot of time. Now Trisha saw through it and she was about to call her out on it.

"I don't remember much from the weekend," Trisha said. "Last thing I remember, I was making out with some guy at the club."

"You don't remember?" Kathy played dumb. "Wow, that's scary, Trish. Honestly, you were acting really weird after that. Like, too loose. If you ask me, I think you might've been roofied. It's a good thing I was there to take you home that night, so at least we know nothing bad happened to you. But you've been complaining about a migraine ever since."

Trisha yawned. "Gosh, that is scary. I'm always so careful! But I guess that might be why I'm so tired."

Kathy nodded, feeling a twinge of guilt for lying to her friend. But offering a note of caution for her partying ways was not necessarily a bad thing. She might not have been roofied this time, but it could've happened. Maybe Trisha would be extra careful in the future.

"Do you need me to help you home so you can rest? You've had a long day."

Trisha nodded slowly, still disoriented. "Yeah, that would be nice."

Kathy helped her friend down the stairs and into the kitchen. She sat her on one of the barstools at the island and offered her a glass of holy water. "Here. Drink this. You'll feel better."

Trisha gulped down the whole glass. "Wow. I'm so thirsty! It's like I haven't had anything to drink in *days*."

"Well, I have more if you want it."

"And I'm starving," Trisha added.

Kathy wondered if the demon had done *anything* human during its possession. Maybe that's why Trisha looked so weak.

"Okay, so how about this: I'll drive you home in your car and we can stop and pick up a pizza on the way."

"That sounds amazing!"

Kathy smiled. She was very glad to have her friend back.

FIND ALL THE BOOKS IN THE COVEN SERIES!

More by the Author

To find more books by the author, visit
DavidNethBooks.com/Books

* * *

Subscribe to his newsletter to be the first to know of new releases and special deals!
DavidNethBooks.com/Newsletter

* * *

If you enjoyed the book, please consider leaving a review on Goodreads or the retailer you bought it from. Reviews help potential readers determine whether they'll enjoy a book, so any comments on what you thought of the story would be very helpful!

About the Author

David Neth is the author of the Coven series, the Under the Moon series, Heat series, the Fuse series, and other stories. He lives in Batavia, NY, where he dreams of a successful publishing career and opening his own bookstore.

Also writes small town romance as D. Allen.

www.DavidNethBooks.com

www.facebook.com/DavidNethBooks